"Caught"
IN THE MIDDLE

Brenda Ford

Author's Tranquility Press
ATLANTA, GEORGIA

Copyright © 2024 by Brenda Ford

All rights reserved. No part of this publication may be reproduced, distributed or transmitted in any form or by any means, including photocopying, recording, or other electronic or mechanical methods, without the prior written permission of the publisher, except in the case of brief quotations embodied in critical reviews and certain other noncommercial uses permitted by copyright law. For permission requests, write to the publisher, addressed "Attention: Permissions Coordinator," at the address below.

Brenda Ford/Author's Tranquility Press
3900 N Commerce Dr. Suite 300 #1255
Atlanta, GA 30344, USA
www.authorstranquilitypress.com

Ordering Information:
Quantity sales. Special discounts are available on quantity purchases by corporations, associations, and others. For details, contact the "Special Sales Department" at the address above.

"Caught" in the Middle / Brenda Ford
Hardback: 978-1-965075-15-9
Paperback: 978-1-964810-72-0
eBook: 978-1-964810-15-7

This book is dedicated to my family for their unwavering support throughout this rewarding endeavor.

PROLOGUE

The early 1990s were difficult years for many inner-city schools. Violent students and hostile parents left school officials struggling to find solutions for toxic situations.

Located in a low-income area, Bradley Middle School showed signs of the same inadequacies as other neighboring educational facilities that were in crisis mode. At Bradley, every teacher, administrator and even the janitorial employees realized that there were overwhelming forces operating against all working personnel in that building. Nevertheless, those odds did not hinder a dedicated staff from trying to overpower the chaotic atmosphere that permeated some of the classrooms. Yes, we definitely had troublemakers that could not be ignored. During these hectic years every school, unfortunately, dealt with its share of student issues. It was a known fact that some schools had more problems than others. Our establishment, for instance, seemed to win "the prize" for housing a bumper crop full of rough necks whose population surpassed all of the other neighborhood schools combined. Cutting classes, disobeying school rules, and causing as much disorder as possible became the daily routine of these hell raisers. It was apparent to all that they did not care about anything or anyone. The fact that the majority of the student body was obedient, well-trained and studious did not supersede the stressful abuse that most of the staff endured from the disgusting actions of a bunch of "Bebe's" kids. Principal Ballentine recognized the need for an additional dean, and repeatedly invited me to apply for the position. Each time he asked, my response was always the same. I informed him that I loved teaching and even though this would be a nice promotion, I wasn't ready to substitute my classroom for an office full of unruly children. I always ended by stating how much I appreciated the confidence he had in my ability to handle such a difficult job. But even I knew that something had to be done soon to bring control into our building.

One day an unforeseen school incident convinced me that the time had come to adjust my views on how I should proceed with my career. Because of the actions of three out of control students, I totally disregarded my inner fears that were accompanied by a little warning voice, and accepted the position as **Dean of Discipline** in what would be considered as one of the roughest middle schools of the decade. Later, when I finally had time to review the past events that caused me to impulsively amend my decision, I conceded that these problem children had suddenly become my responsibility. My peaceful life at Bradley Middle School would never be the same.

CHAPTER 1

The dawning of my new career began on a brisk autumn day in October. Pausing to gaze around the block, I stepped out of my car at Bradley Middle School. Decay was visible everywhere. Boarded up houses and abandoned cars were evident throughout the neighborhood. Nevertheless, the autumn leaves falling in the early morning breeze gave this community an atmosphere of beauty that was seldom seen during the other seasons. I closed the car door automatically, still deeply immersed in thought. Today was the day before Halloween. It appeared that the kids had begun celebrating early. Signs of this spooky holiday were everywhere. At least the "trick" part of the festivities was coming along very nicely for the rabble-rousers. Broken bottles and busted balloons, which had been filled with colorful dyes and dried broken eggs, were strewn across the sidewalk up and down the block. Remnants of this spree were also seen splashed on the side of the school, overlapping the graffiti that had become part of the building's decor. As I walked toward the entrance, I became aware of a group of boys in the schoolyard huddled together. Togetherness with this bunch was obviously not a good sign. I could detect trouble . . . big trouble generating from the urgency in their expressive faces. Filing this scene in the back of my mind, I quickly entered the building.

CHAPTER 2

The main hallway was busy with faculty members, parents and students moving about. School had been in session for six weeks and Mr. Ballentine still had not hired a second dean. He had asked me twice to take the position, but I had my reasons for not wanting to "mix it up" with these kids. A dean's life was a hard life. Most of the time deans only became involved with the bad students. Those were the students that had habitual disciplinary problems. Their attitudes stunk, and they didn't give a damn about anyone or anything. They would curse you out in a second without blinking an eye. When you tried to get support from their parents or guardians, you'd find that the adult's mind-set might be worse than their children's. **No thank you!** Don't get me wrong, I appreciated being considered for the position, but I preferred to remain in my classroom, teach my classes, and try to stay out of unnecessary lines of fire. Though, I must admit I was flattered to know the head man thought enough of my skills to offer me the job. *Well, maybe . . . Forget it, Betty Jean!* As I clocked in, I tried to change my thoughts toward the day's plans.

The memo advertising the dean's position glared back at me from above the time clock.

"Don't tell me that you're still refusing to give this fantastic position any consideration?" A friendly voice from behind asked the question that all inquiring minds in the school were dying to know.

I knew he had to be kidding when he described the dean's job as being "fantastic." I also knew that his reason for asking was the result of Betty Jean being the topic of discussion for the past few weeks. My colleagues were trying very hard to convince me to accept the position. The school needed an additional dean and my friends felt that I was the best person to handle the post. *Huh... a lot they knew!* The faculty in this educational establishment was just like any other nosy family. The busybodies considered juicy tidbits about any of the faculty fair game. During lunch they would combine the gossipy news of the day with discussions about lesson plans and disruptive students. But the natives were restless for something new, and I was it.

"Yes, I am."

I answered as I turned and came face to face with "Action Jackson" smiling down at me. He earned that nickname because he acted "bad" like the character in the movie "Action Jackson". He held the other dean's position and always seemed to be prepped and ready for action whenever there was trouble. Everyone knew that Action Jackson handled most fights and arguments with a strong hand. We also were aware that his manner of controlling these situations worked. It appeared that he relished his nickname. Maybe it was because his first name was really Marion. With a name like that I guess most men would prefer the name "Action" too.

"I must admit, though, I had been giving the dean's job some thought lately. Maybe the idea was beginning to appeal to me."

"Well," he said with a smile, "I think you would make a great dean. These kids need a strong person like you in their corner. Plus, being a woman, you would probably be a good mother figure to some of the students on the 4th floor. Also, let's not forget that since we are without another dean, I have the misfortune of handling all the grades by myself. Believe me, that's no fun. So, please hurry and take the job, lady, I need help!"

Amused at his display of desperation, I thanked him for his vote of confidence and headed for my classroom.

CHAPTER 3

Friends and colleagues agreed that I was the homeroom teacher for one of the most difficult 8th grade classes in the school. One good reason could be that many of the female students in my homeroom outweighed the males. They were huge! Some of my fourteen-year-olds weighed over 200 pounds and a few might have been almost six feet. After observing my girls during an altercation with students from another class, a male colleague playfully described them as looking like female linebackers on a football team. Okay, that remark was a little harsh! And it didn't help that their gruff personalities were sometimes misinterpreted as uncooperative behavior. Guess what? They were not alone. The rest of my class's conduct wasn't much better. But they were my students and although most of them might have a few problems, I still enjoyed teaching them. The morning passed quickly, and the 8th grader's lunch hour arrived. I dismissed my class to the cafeteria by the side exit and I took a quicker route using the back stairs.

    The minute I entered the stairwell I knew that I had made a big mistake. There was a loud commotion from above that I immediately assessed as trouble. It was obvious that I was listening to a fight in progress. It was also apparent that there weren't any security guards or teachers around. Undoubtedly, that was why the students chose this area. It was secluded and allowed them to do their damage in private. I could tell that the dispute was between girls which made matters much worse. Girls were not the type to "forgive and forget." They refuse to listen if an adult tries to reason with them, and they get a rise out of trying to tear one another apart verbally and physically. I'd rather deal with boys any day.

"Fuck you, bitch!"

Those words loudly bellowed down the stairs to my ears. Great! Now, I felt I had no choice but to intervene. Halfheartedly, I turned and headed up to the third floor. The argument must have been going on for quite some time because the verbal assaults were over. Now, it had become physical. Somehow, I managed to push myself between the two students which was a *colossal* mistake. They locked their arms around me, entangling their fingers into each other's hair. Then they began striking around me with whatever appendage was available. Arms and feet swatted and kicked through the air. All three of us almost tumbled down the stairs as I struggled to maintain my balance. Holding tightly to the banister, I managed to remain upright and prevented an even bigger catastrophe.

CHAPTER 4

"Why didn't I wear my sneakers today?" I muttered to myself.

They were still holding on to each other's hair while tightly wrapped around my waist. Obviously, neither student was concerned about the large figure struggling in the middle. Thank goodness this staircase led directly to the cafeteria. I knew that I could get help once I reached the first floor. However, additional problems now existed. By now there was a large group of students following us down the stairs and a larger crowd waiting for our arrival at the bottom. I considered this double trouble. Kids loved a fight. This was their in-school entertainment. To some, it was better than an interesting television show or even a rap video. A good school fight could go a long way. For instance, after the spectators discussed who won, which would sometimes be a matter of opinion, they would then dissect the incident by debating who made the best moves or who landed the most punches; which one had the most clothes on after it was over; and who had the largest support group of friends cheering them on. The list goes on and on. This argument could be prolonged for days with both sides finding fresh facts to fuel the debate from fellow onlookers.

"I'll kill you, bitch," one young lady screamed as we reached the first floor.

"Just try, slut. You ain't nuttin' but a fuckin' ho'! You ain't killing nobody," the other girl responded.

By now both girls were tired and out of breath. I could tell that they were just showing off for their audience and would be glad to end it all. Noticing the cheering section surrounding them, each fighter found renewed energy and intensified the battle to gain points for her win. Meanwhile, I was still busy trying to separate them from around my waist. Pushing on the one I was facing was not working. They still had their hands tangled in each other's hair. Hair extensions were everywhere. As we descended to the first floor, the mess had fallen on the stairs as well as in a circle around us as they continued their brutal assault on each other.

"Oh boy, am I in a predicament," I said aloud and maybe with a little too much intensity. I was worried that neither combatant was concerned about injuring the person caught in the middle of their physical dispute. I needed help because these young ladies weren't loosening their grip. Suddenly, the lunchroom door swung open and Mr. Johnson, an assistant principal, rushed to my assistance. Unfortunately, before he could reach me something flew through the air and struck him in the eye. It came in the direction of the crowd which was on the verge of becoming an uncontrollable mob. Poor Mr. Johnson toppled to the floor like a log.

"Ooooh," a chorus of voices yelled from the bystanders in response to the attack. As the item smashed on the ground, I could see that he was hit with a frozen egg. At that time, a hand shot out from the crowd, and a fist landed a hard blow on my right jaw. My eyes quickly moved in that direction just in time to see Thomas, a student in one of my 8th grade classes, pull back his hand.

"Ooooh," echoed the expanding crowd for the second time much louder and with added excitement in their voices because now a new thrill was added to the mix. A female teacher was assaulted.

"Where are those doggone security guards?" I muttered, noticing that my voice was beginning to sound panicky.

We had four members of the security team in our school, but it seemed like much less. They were never around when you needed them. Mr. Johnson required help and could be seriously hurt. Furthermore, other students were getting involved in this mess. If help didn't come soon, this was going to turn into a "free for all." So far, I wasn't seriously injured. However, by the way things were progressing, that could change at any second. Suddenly, the pressure around my waist began to loosen. I turned to see Action Jackson pulling on the girl behind me. Words could not express how happy I was to see him. I continued to push the other girl in front of me. Finally, with our combined efforts we succeeded in pulling them apart.

CHAPTER 5

Now that the fight was over, I looked around and evaluated the damage. The aftermath of this brawl was an upsetting sight to view. As you could guess, hair extensions littered the entire hallway. Honestly, there was almost as much hair on the floor as on the fighters' heads. Both girls had their blouses ripped off. One girl was holding her bra to help cover up her breasts because both straps were useless. They were torn and dangling at her sides. Mr. Johnson was standing by the stairs with an ice bag on his eye while being supported by the school nurse. What a tragedy! Action Jackson had a hold of the two girls and was heading towards Mr. Ballentine's office.

The entertainment had ended, and the crowd slowly moved back to the cafeteria. They had wanted more and were disappointed that additional blood, besides the few scratches on the girls, wasn't forthcoming. Thomas, the boy who punched me, was walking away with his friends. Overwhelmed with anger, I grabbed his arm as he was about to pass me.

"You're coming with me," I said, spinning him around to face me.

"What for? I ain't do nuttin'," he responded giving his arm a slight yank in a useless attempt to free himself from my grasp.

"Nothing? Is that what you called that punch you gave me . . . nothing?" I yelled. "Well, pay close attention. This is how I handle "nothings."

Our heated conversation continued as I practically dragged him toward Mr. Ballentine's office.

"That wasn't me that hit you. You got the wrong kid, lady."

"That lie isn't going to fly with me," I replied through clenched teeth.

"I saw you," I said looking him in the eye. Then I delivered the words I knew he didn't want to hear but made me feel 100% better.

"Congratulations, that punch will get you a five-day suspension. Your own personal vacation from school," I yelled angrily.

"You ain't no dean," he shot back. "You can't suspend me and I ain't going with you. **Let me go,**" he shouted as he tried to pull his arm from me once again.

"Let me explain to you just how this is going to work." Again, I spoke to him through clenched teeth but this time in a whisper. "You can come along peacefully, or if you cause trouble, I will settle this the hard way by taking one of your body parts with me to the office. Any part will do. But some piece of you will be coming with me today! It's your choice."

With those words I stopped walking and turned so he could observe my expression while he digested my words. I was angry enough to physically do combat with him and he knew it. By now we had reached the office where Mr. Ballentine appeared in his doorway. He was alerted by Action Jackson that I was on my way to deliver a student who had punched me. We were at the end of our staring match when reality finally hit Thomas. He knew that he had lost this battle and was not going to escape punishment. Grudgingly, he did the next best thing that any teenager could do to salvage whatever dignity he had left. Shrugging his shoulders, he put on his "bad" walk and swaggered slowly behind Mr. Ballentine into his office, each arm swinging alternately behind his back. What a sight! If I wasn't so angry about what happened to me, I would have been able to appreciate how ridiculous his saunter looked. Turning to leave I announced to the principal in a loud voice, mostly for Thomas' benefit.

"By the way, Mr. Ballentine, I've got good news for you. I've decided to accept the dean's position. Also, I gave Thomas a five-day suspension and would like to see his parents after he has completed his days at home."

Mr. Ballentine smiled happily, giving me a nod to let me know he agreed with my change of heart. A satisfied feeling overcame me as I exited the office knowing I **now** had the power to execute that suspension. Thomas was right, I thought to myself. I wasn't dean at the time I issued his punishment, so I could not legally have suspended him. But he forced my hand. My suspension was legal now. And it gave me great pleasure to be the person that executed the order.

Unfortunately, we couldn't find a witness to the attack on Mr. Johnson, and no one would admit to throwing the egg. My mind suddenly remembered the group of boys I saw in the schoolyard this morning. Thomas was part of that little cluster. Recalling his presence now made me wonder if attacking teachers was part of the plans they were so busily discussing.

Before the end of the day, news about Betty Jean Lawson becoming the new dean spread throughout the entire school. Even the students were approaching me with the question, "You the new dean, Mrs. Lawson?" I answered all the students' questions and with reservations expressed appreciation for the congratulatory remarks offered by my colleagues.

To reinforce a previous statement, I maintain that the majority of our students were well behaved and smart students who wanted an education and were respectful to their teachers. On the other hand, as dean, the majority of my time would be spent with the other students that didn't want to learn and who spent their time and energy preventing their classmates from receiving an education in a calm and safe environment. This is why the dean's job is important. We deal, first hand, with those students who cause trouble in the school.

Leaving school that day I experienced for the first time in my life an alarming feeling of mental fatigue.

"Thank God it's Friday," I bellowed as I walked to my car wondering if I had made the right choice by allowing my emotions to overrule sound judgment.

I looked forward to the weekend knowing it would give me time to pamper my sore jaw as well as process, with some skepticism, my hasty decision. Who could have guessed that the actions of three students would so quickly influence me into making this career move? As I slowly drove home, I realized that I was going to be in for a very long and stressful year.

CHAPTER 6

I spent the next few weeks becoming acquainted with my new position. During this period, I saw Thomas' mother who was very cooperative. She guaranteed that her son would cause no more problems in school and apologized for Thomas' bad behavior. It was a pleasure to meet such a supportive parent and I thanked her for her help. I felt lucky to have had such a pleasant experience for my first parent conference. Unfortunately, future events did not all go so smoothly.

A week after accepting my position, a new teacher named Josey Taylor was hired to take over my daily classes. I knew that time was going to be allotted from my schedule for me to help her acclimate into the routine of dealing with lesson plans and overzealous 8th graders. Upon meeting this young lady, I became a little worried. My immediate impression of her was that she talked too fast, smiled too much and probably lacked the experience needed to handle this age group, especially my high-spirited class. After a short interview I surmised my feelings about her capabilities were most likely accurate. She told me that she had just spent home room period with my students before coming to my office. As we chatted, I observed her body language. The smile that appeared to be permanently painted on her face didn't fool me at all. I could see that the visit with my class left her noticeably nervous and possibly even a little frightened of them. With these kids, a teacher needed to be serious in order to portray confidence. She needed to get rid of that smile. This definitely was not good.

Her smile stimulated my memory into remembering a day in the past when I had just completed my first year as a teacher at Bradley. My students never knew I had teeth until today, which was approximately twenty-six hours before school closed for the summer vacation. I vaguely remember a funny incident occurring in the classroom while the students were helping me put books and other school supplies away for safe keeping. I can't momentarily recall the actual episode, but whatever it was that took place inspired me to laugh. Hearing me chuckle, the entire class stopped what they were doing and stared at me in silence. In turn, the sudden silence prompted me to stop laughing and look around the room to see if there was a problem of which I was not aware; only to find out that **I . . . was the problem.** You see, I had a reputation as a no-nonsense teacher to maintain. This meant, I very seldom smiled, and I definitely never laughed. In Bradley too much grinning in the presence of students could be misconstrued as being weak or soft. That type of negative reputation would travel around the building like the plague, thus rendering a teacher ineffective. So, the sight of their instructor suddenly acting "normal" seemed to traumatize every last one of them. Realizing that I was the reason for their bewilderment made me laugh even harder. I really roared then. My poor confused class, looking around at one another, stood quietly watching as their teacher reveled in her happy moment. I fondly remember that day. As a new educator with only one year of experience, I consider that moment one of the highlights of my teaching career.

Returning my thoughts to the present, I realized that I was not paying attention to what Josey was saying. Checking her out again, I concluded that her fast talking was most likely due to anxiety. My goodness, she needs to calm down! If she can't get her jitters under control, this would definitely inhibit her effectiveness as an instructor.

Middle school kids can smell fear of a teacher a mile away. They are specialists in using this ability to take advantage of most circumstances. Mentally I debated whether I should discuss my concerns with Mr. Ballentine. I hated to think that my lack of confidence in Josey's abilities might cause her to lose this job. So, I did the next best thing. Before the end of our visit, I gave her a "crash course" on class control and additional information about some of the problem students that were in my other classes. She had four other classes to instruct daily besides my homeroom. As she rose from the chair and prepared to leave, I wanted to warn her about so many other obstacles she might be facing. But I knew she had to learn some things for herself. Experience was the best teacher and confronting her fears would enhance her survival skills. Therefore, all I said was . . .

"Anytime you need me, I'm here to help you. But you *must* get rid of that smile, Josey. It will only bring you problems that you cannot control."

"I've smiled my entire life, Betty, I don't know if I can stop now. All I can promise you is that I'll try."

With those words, she walked across the room and opened the door. The last sight I saw before she closed the door was her face featuring a big smile as she turned to wave goodbye.

Pushing that nagging feeling aside, I decided to wait and see if my replacement could pull her act together. With a little time and some help from me, she just might be able to hold her own in the trenches. I made a mental note to check in on her frequently. One month should do it. By then she would have either conquered the students or they would have methodically annihilated her. If the latter took place, I would not have to say anything about her job performance because she would probably be leaving in a hurry. Unconsciously, I crossed my fingers for luck, hoping no one would ask me how I felt my protege was doing. I didn't want to lie about her expertise, only to have my words come back to haunt me. Unfortunately, her day of accountability came sooner than I expected.

CHAPTER 7

It was the beginning of my third week as dean. Looking back, my first two weeks were not as bad as I had anticipated. They passed quickly with only a few minor incidents. I couldn't believe my good fortune. As I rushed into the office of my colleague, Janelle St. Patrick, I found it difficult to contain my enthusiasm. Janell was the 7th and 8th grade guidance counselor. Her days were filled with parent conferences, student mediations and district meetings. She was one of the best counselors in the school district and one of my biggest supporters. As a member of the educational team, I valued her friendship as well as her opinion.

"Things are looking good! Maybe this will be the year that most of our disorderly students take a vacation from disruptive behavior," I said happily squeezing her shoulder.

"Don't you believe it," she responded quickly. "I've been around for a long time. After you've been dean for a while you too will begin to get a feel for trouble. If that Halloween incident that you were involved in was any indication of events to come, I can guarantee that the students will be just as active as all the other years . . . maybe even more so."

Janell was definitely a great person to talk to. I enjoyed visiting with her even if it was only for a few minutes. Our jobs also coincided from time to time. I would supply the necessary information to her about a difficult student that needed her guidance, and she would return the favor whenever the opportunity presented itself.

"I have an appointment with a parent in about thirty seconds. Maybe you would like to stay and meet her. Chances are you will be running into Mrs. Jones and her son, Richard, in the future. He will most likely be one of our most frequent visitors."

Just as Janell finished her sentence, the door opened, and a tired looking woman walked into the room. She was accompanied by a tall, lanky young man about fourteen years old and a young child in a stroller. The scowl on Richard's face told me that he was not pleased to be here. What an angry young man, was my immediate impression upon being introduced. Janell was right; this teenager spelled trouble. The door opened again and Josey Taylor, still smiling, nervously walked into the room. Her eyes darted from side to side trying to take in everything in a single glance and finally they rested on Richard. The tension in the room was palpable. I picked up on a dirty look transmitted from Richard towards Josey's direction that made a shiver go down my spine. Did Janell see this, too? I certainly hope so. A teacher needs to be cognizant of signals that students emit among themselves and to other adults. Sometimes that insight can prevent a catastrophe. I wondered what happened to bring this group together for a meeting. I also wondered why Josey hadn't mentioned to me that she was having trouble with a student. I could only assume that she wanted to see if she could handle the situation alone, which was promising. Whatever the reason, I was happy to see her use the initiative to move forward with this student. However, I was troubled that I had never seen Richard before. Since Josey had my old class, this youngster's unfamiliar face could only mean that he was a new student. Damn, just one week on the job and she had to run into this. What rotten luck! When they placed Richard in Josey's class, they must have forgotten that she was a new teacher. Changing my mind by reconsidering my original analysis of this situation, I concluded that maybe trying to handle this young man alone was not such a good idea. If she had only confided in me the first time she had problems with her new student, I could have had him transferred out of her class before he became a bigger problem. Waiting to see if conditions will get better or go away never works. They only fester and end up getting worse. Unfortunately, it's too late to do anything about it now. I told Josey and Janell that I would see them later, then turned and nodded a goodbye to Richard's mother. With an uneasy feeling that I couldn't dismiss, I left the room and headed for my office.

CHAPTER 8

As I walked down the hall, it was hard for me to discount the look I saw in Richard's eyes when he stared at Josey. I don't think I've ever seen so much hatred in just one glance, especially from a child. I stopped briefly to send three students to class who were loitering in the halls, and by the time I reached my office the late bell was ringing. I froze when I heard the bell continue to ring signaling a secret warning to the staff that there is a major problem in the building.

"Brinnnng, brinnnng,-brinng," two long, a pause then one short ring. That is the signal that means there is trouble on the third floor. I had just left Janell's office which was located on that same floor. That's funny . . . I didn't notice any problems. Except for those students I sent to class, the halls were pretty quiet.

The bell began to ring again. Two long pauses and a short, two long a pause and a short. Teachers began to appear in their doorways.

"What's going on? What happened? Mrs. Lawson, do you know what the problem is?" Questions were coming from all directions. Unfortunately, I couldn't answer any of them.

All I could do was shrug my shoulders and hope that we would find out soon. Like I expected we didn't have long to wait. Mr. Ballentine's voice came in loud and clear over the speakers.

"There is a double-parked car that needs to be moved. The tag number is FFF643. Please move it immediately."

I recognized that the number was really 346 but being reported backwards just in case students notice it was a code or signal. Ballentine repeated the message, but I wasn't listening. I was too busy running down the stairs to the third floor. That was Janell St. Patrick's office. The coded message stated that all security was to report to her room without wasting any time. What in the world could have happened in such a short period that would have caused the principal to send out an emergency message?

When I reached Janell's office, I found guards at her door taking turns looking through the small glass window. Without excusing myself, I pushed my way to the front of the group. Only Janell and Josey were visible and both ladies were looking toward a section of the room that couldn't be seen from the door. A young male's voice, which I assumed was Richard's, could be heard.

"I'm gonna kill all you mother fuckas. Back off or you'll force me to do it now."

Janell signaled to us to stay where we were by slightly moving her head back and forth. All of a sudden my friend began to reason with Richard and her voice turned to silk. Listening to her speak with that comforting tone gave me confidence in her ability to successfully handle this rising crisis. Janell started by referring to Richard's mother as his best friend.

"If you harm your mom you won't have anyone to turn to when you need help, comfort and even love. Then, what about your little brother? Who would raise him if you seriously injured your mother? You certainly wouldn't be able to do it because you would be in jail."

Richard replied, "He'll be okay."

Was I mistaken or was he crying? His wavering voice gave me hope that Janell might be winning this battle. She played her winning card when she said,

"If you hurt anyone in this room, I can almost guarantee that you'll probably spend the rest of your life in prison and your brother won't be okay. Chances are he will have a troublesome life with his mother dead and his brother locked away for the crime. Richard, you might have a few problems. Everyone in the world has problems. But, I don't think you want to resort to violence. Your mom needs you. You're a smart boy and I'm sure you know that you can't help her from prison."

I could hear big sobs coming from the concealed area of the room. At that moment Janell moved forward out of my sight. When she re-emerged, she was holding an ice pick in her hand.

Josey did not move throughout this entire incident. In fact, I had forgotten she was there. When I finally looked at her, I noticed her face had lost its pleasant expression and all of the color had drained. She was lopsidedly leaning on the desk for support. Then, without a sound, she sank to the floor. At once Janell opened the door for the security guards to take Richard into custody and passed off the ice pick. I rushed into her office and both Janell and I tried to revive Josey. Mr. Ballentine soon entered along with Mrs. Bertram, the school nurse. Mrs. Bertram tried to rouse her, but to no avail. So, she pulled a small capsule out of her pocket and broke it open under her nose. Turns out Mrs. Bertram had grabbed some smelling salts out of the first aid kit. Josey quickly awakened, fighting to stand up. We held her down and tried to keep her quiet until she was alert enough to move about.

CHAPTER 9

News about the events that happened in Janell's office hit the halls in record time. The whole building heard how this new student pulled out a weapon and threatened his mother. Rumor was he became angry with her after she contacted the school officials concerning his threatening behavior with family members. He felt his mom was betraying him by putting his business out in the neighborhood. But that was not Mrs. Jones' intentions. She said she didn't know who to turn to for help and was hoping the school would know what to do. She claimed that Richard was physically abusive to her and she couldn't take it anymore. Richard's reaction to her cry for help was the ice pick episode. We also found out that he had issues of hatred relating to women. It would have been beneficial to all concerned if we had received information on this student before he physically appeared, especially regarding these dangerous personality traits that would make him explode. We never would have had only women in that room if we had known it could set him off.

Crying hysterically, Mrs. Jones was escorted from the third floor to Mr. Ballentine's office. From there she was taken in a police car to see her son who had been arrested. Josey was transported to the hospital for observation. She never returned to Bradley Middle School again, not even to get her personal property or clean out her desk. I had anticipated her employment being a short one. However, not even I could have predicted that it would have ended with such turmoil. Richard Jones was removed from the school in handcuffs. After his release from jail, he was confined for only three days in a mental hospital. Customarily, dangerous students are transferred to an alternative school or learning facility when released from an institution. This is usually an establishment especially designed for troubled youngsters. We knew Richard was deeply disturbed and needed more than three days of psychological evaluation to diagnose and cure his demons. But since our establishment was not equipped to handle students who were volatile, we all figured we'd never see him again. However, one day while making my rounds in the halls, I saw a tall, lanky figure approaching. To my dismay, it was Richard Jones.

CHAPTER 10

Having Richard back in our school was certainly no picnic. His surprise appearance threatened to spoil my Thanksgiving holiday. I had no peace after his return. I constantly worried about his explosive temper, which might happen at any time. Who knows . . . next time I could be the recipient of his wrath. No one was safe. Janell confided in me that the doctors at the psychiatric clinic felt it was fine for him to return to school. His personal doctor felt that his outburst was just a childish cry for attention. Even though they thought it was probably a once in a lifetime break down, no one could guarantee that it wouldn't happen again. Consequently, we were told that if we saw any signs of a recurring outburst, we were to call them immediately. Good grief . . . that definitely didn't sound reassuring. And who were they kidding. We all knew that, most likely, Richard would have a problem of this nature again. I'm sure his doctors knew it, too. In my opinion, those medical professionals gave the most ridiculous prognosis that I have ever heard.

Anyway, now that Richard had become our problem for a second time, troubles had already begun. He was constantly walking the halls. This meant security, Action Jackson, and I were very much involved in keeping him calm. Richard was an eighth grader which was Action's grade. However, he never hung out on the second floor. He seemed to prefer, my corridor, the fourth floor. As a result, I had the risky task of confronting him daily. So far he was very cooperative at all of our encounters. Whenever I spoke to him about being out of his class and on the wrong floor, he would apologize and head for the stairs. Nevertheless, his polite facade didn't prevent my nerves from jumping through the roof. Where Richard was concerned, I was always waiting for the other shoe to fall. And I figured that it was only a matter of time before it did. We were informed that his calm demeanor was due to medication. Thank goodness for meds! May help reach us in time the day he forgets or refuses to take them. Our frequent encounters continued for six more days and then he disappeared from school.

We found out that shortly before Thanksgiving, Richard was transferred to another school. Words cannot express my euphoric feeling. Winning the lottery couldn't have felt better. Later that day I was also brought up to date on Mrs. Jones' moving from the neighborhood to protect her son. She expressed concern that he was being persecuted by his peers. The neighborhood's report had it that the truth of the matter was not entirely the way she described. Students' account was that the neighbors and kids on his block did not persecute him. They just avoided him. They felt they couldn't trust his explosive temperament. For that reason, none of his friends' parents would allow him to come into their homes. Richard became very depressed about the circumstances surrounding his life. Mrs. Jones decided that her son needed a fresh start in a place where no one knew his past. They left for parts unknown. Wherever they went I hope his mother obtained for him the counseling necessary to help him grow up to be a successfully productive human being, for his sake as well as everyone he encounters, including her. We all, at Bradley Middle School, wished him the best in his new environment.

CHAPTER 11

Thanksgiving came and went uneventfully. Water glasses clinked together in celebration around the lunch table as my colleagues and I congratulated ourselves on keeping the peace for the entire week prior to the holiday. Even though we were patting each other on the back, we knew that this stroke of good luck was greatly due to the students who were on their best behavior. Our youngsters made sure not to do anything which might result in being grounded for the entire four-day vacation; being grounded means no fun.

Seeing that this was our first day back after the holiday, I was a little apprehensive about how the day would end. Today might be the day that everything hits the fan. Prior to the long weekend, Action Jackson alerted me to a possible gang problem that might be developing in the neighborhood. This could mean trouble for the school.

Often gang issues are not confined to their perspective blocks or neighborhoods. Instead, they find a way onto school grounds and even into the classrooms. By 1:00 p.m. we received incredibly wonderful news; the gang war was broken up by undercover cops and the leaders were arrested. We realized that we had dodged a big bullet this time. I can't understand why kids don't seem to care about the horrible devastation going on throughout their communities from their stupid fights and rumbles that cause innocent people to get hurt, sometimes even killed. Thinking back, memories of a similar situation loomed in my mind of an incident that occurred a few years ago.

CHAPTER 12

Halfway through the 2nd period on this particular day, the classroom door swung open. It was done with such force that the door hit the wall and in bouncing back would have automatically slammed shut except for the figure standing in its path. Positioned in the doorway, a tough looking kid irritably scanned the room.

"Oh shit," a male voice muttered from the back of the room.

"Damn it man . . . He's not here," a different voice bellowed from the other side of the class.

I took a good look at the young man effectively posing in the entrance. He wasn't a large boy; in fact, he was rather small in stature. But it was obvious that his size was not an inconvenience.

And apparently his mere presence terrorized my class. Wide eyes stared at the figure that stood silently in the entrance. He clearly enjoyed the response that he received from the nervous students. You could tell that what he lacked in size he definitely made up for instance. Needing to find out what he wanted, I started to rise from my desk. My intentions were to also stop him from entering any further into the room. A gentle pressure on my shoulder caused me to remain seated. Looking up expecting a really good explanation from the person pushing me back in my seat, I saw Billy who was glaring down at me with stern eyes. I had forgotten that he was at my desk asking a question before the door opened. Once more I directed my attention back to the youngster in the doorway. It seemed as if I was not important to him; in fact, he acted like I wasn't there. Ignoring my presence gave Billy the opportunity to whisper in my ear without being seen.

"Don't get up and don't say nuttin' Ms. Lawson. He ain't nobody to get tough with. He's bad news. Just sit still and keep your mouth shut."

Billy's voice had the urgency of a sergeant giving a member of his troops an order. My first impulse was to ignore Billy's warning and throw this insolent young man out of my classroom. How dare he just burst into my room like that! I was about to give him a piece of my mind when he spoke again.

"Tell him I'm looking for him. I ain't gonna wait forever. Y'all let him know that he better bring his ass to the meeting place tonight or he ain't gonna have an ass to bring to no place no mo."

He stepped back and the door slammed shut. My entire class was visibly upset. Everyone knew who that person was, everyone but me. Turning to Billy who was still standing by my desk with his hand on my shoulder, I asked,

"Who in the world was that?"

"You don't wanna know," he responded.

"Yes, I do. When a student walks into my classroom and acts like he owns the place, I want to know everything about him."

"First of all, Ms. Lawson, he's known on our block as Jason. I don't know his last name, only his first. Also, he's a drug dealer, not a student. Rumor is that he and Jeremy's been having beef with each other for weeks. They say he wants to hurt him bad. The word around the neighborhood is he probably wants to kill him. Look, Ms. Lawson, I think you're a okay teacher. I couldn't let you get up 'cause you would be hurt. I'm sure Jason was packing. He carries a 9 mil. all the time and he don't care who knows it. If you ask me, he likes people to know he's bad and dangerous. Nobody messes with him, not even the cops."

I thought about what Billy said for a few seconds then suddenly remembered that Jeremy has not been to class for a while.

"Is Jason the reason why Jeremy hasn't been to school for two days?"

"Yeah," Billy sadly said nodding his head. "He also ain't been around the block for a couple of days. The last time I saw him was last Friday. I was worried that Jason had caught up with him. Seeing him here today gives me hope that Jeremy's still among the living."

I sent a student with a note to the principal warning him of an intruder roaming the halls. As far as I knew he was still in the building and could be going from class to class looking for Jeremy. My class was visibly upset. Knowing their state of mind, it would be useless to continue the lesson, so I allowed them to quietly talk for the remainder of the period. As expected, their conversations were all about what had just happened. When the period ended, I notified the office, security guards and Action Jackson of the bad blood between the two boys. It could become a school problem if they tried to settle their feud in the building.

Luckily, we never had to deal with those boys again. Jeremy never came back to class. I heard that his mother had sent him out of the state hoping this whole problem would blow over. Two weeks later Billy informed me that Jason eventually caught up with Jeremy. Jeremy had snuck into town to see his friends. His mother didn't even know he was back in the area.

It came as no surprise to me to find out that Jason will probably receive life in prison without the possibility of parole for the murder of Jeremy Cintron. What a terrible, terrible tragedy!

CHAPTER 13

December came in with a bang. Already the festivities for Christmas were all around town. As expected, these celebrations became more frequent as we got closer to the "big" day. "Tis' The Season To Be Jolly." Students and teachers were both making a concerted effort to live up to this slogan and get along with one another prior to the holiday. With extra encouragement from the staff for the students to repeat last month's good behavior, we all had high expectations of peaceful weeks to come. Thanksgiving had passed without a hitch, and we hoped that the Christmas tidings would be just as kind. Liberation day was just around the horizon. Only twenty-three more days until teachers' salvation! Then a ten-day vacation full of peace and quiet would become all mine. I could hardly wait.

When I entered the students' cafeteria, I was greeted by Mr. Johnson. We both were scheduled to cover third period lunch duty this year. However, since I became dean, this was our first coverage together. He had been absent since Halloween because of the frozen egg incident. Giving him a big hug, I told him how delighted I was to see him. He thanked me for my warm welcome and then changed the conversation to the upcoming holiday season.

"Wow!" he exclaimed. "Seems like the kids have the holiday spirit. I hope this exhilarated atmosphere continues so that we can have a peaceful ending to this year."

Mr. Johnson's remark took me by surprise. I had completely forgotten that January was only a month away. Where did the time go?

"Yep, the mood appears to be tranquil," I replied with a sigh. "We made it through Thanksgiving and with a little luck, we'll make it through Christmas."

Switching the conversation to his health, I questioned him on his eye injury. "I've been anxious to find out how you've been doing. How is your eye?"

"Much better," he said, "but for a while I was worried. My sight was constantly blurred for quite some time and seemed to be taking too long to clear up. Right now, it's not too bad, but that could change any minute. The clarity comes and goes. Anyway, I am thankful for this much. A month ago, there weren't any moments that my eye was in focus. The doctor said the progress my eye is making is a good sign. He is confident that eventually my vision will permanently return. So, I guess I will have to be patient."

He had barely completed his sentence when we heard a loud noise that caused everyone to freeze in their present positions. Mr. Johnson and I scanned the cafeteria looking to see if the source of the noise was in the room. Students were also noticeably shaken by the loud noise and stopped eating and talking.

"What was that?" Mr. Johnson and I said simultaneously. Within fifteen seconds after we spoke, we could hear students asking the same question. But no answer was forthcoming. If you asked me, it sounded like a bomb had detonated close by. Since it was not in our immediate area, I figured it must have come from the front of our building. Walking to the window I cautiously peeked out from the side, making sure I didn't expose too much of my body. Getting hit in the face with a projectile was a possibility if whatever it was that exploded wasn't finished with whatever it was doing.

"Where's Mrs. Lawson?' I heard Mr. Ballentine's voice asking for me from across the room. "Over here," I yelled walking to meet him halfway. The kids all turned to see what the principal wanted with me. Noticing the sudden interest in our conversation, Mr. Ballentine lowered his voice to a whisper.

"You're needed outside. Somehow your car was involved in an accident."

"*My car was involved in a **what**?* How could that happen? It's still parked, isn't it?" I whispered back.

I was firing questions faster than he could answer. My mouth was open to ask another question when he stopped me.

"I don't know any more than what I told you. I'll cover for you here. Go find out what happened."

CHAPTER 14

Leaving the building at a fast pace, I walked quickly out the front door and into the middle of a crime in progress. Police cars were everywhere. There were patrol cars, unmarked detective cars, and a few other cars that were unidentifiable. At least ten cars pointing in different directions were scattered throughout the block. Looking over in the direction where I had parked, my eyes rested on an unbelievable sight. The front, the back and the top of my car were smashed. Incredibly, the car parked in front of mine was in worse condition. Resembling an automobile that had taken part in a demolition derby, it was totally destroyed by a strange car that was balancing upside down on its roof top.

"What in the world happened here?" I mumbled, not expecting a response. As I walked towards my car I was approached by an officer.

"Are you the owner of this car?" he asked pointing to my blue Chevy.

"Yes, I am," I replied. "Jeez, look at what was done to my vehicle! Who's responsible for this?" I said nodding in the direction of the two cars. Brrrrr, it was cold outside! Suddenly noticing the icy chill in the air, I wrapped my arms around my body. When I ran out of the school, I forgot to get my coat. I didn't stop to think about the cold weather. My only objective was to find out what happened to my car. The weatherman said that the temperature was 16 degrees this morning. It couldn't be more than 20 degrees now. It's freezing out here! A voice interrupted my thoughts. It was the policeman again.

"This car over here," he said jerking his head to the left, "hit your car, and somehow ended up on top of the car parked in front of yours. I'm sorry I can't give you any more information because I just got here. So you'll have to ask somebody else for more details."

Thanking him for his information, I glanced past him just in time to get a glimpse of a detective putting a handcuffed teenage boy into the back of a police car. He looked so young, maybe around fourteen. Tears were streaming down his cheeks and he appeared petrified about his predicament. I wondered who he was and what part he played in wrecking the cars. As I carefully studied his face, I did not recognize him as one of our students. Changing my focal point to an approaching person, I realized the policeman who spoke to me a few minutes ago was back.

"We would like you to come down to the station later to make out a report."

I told him I would be there after work, if not sooner. I then returned my attention back to continue analyzing my car's damages. Gazing at my poor means of transportation for another five minutes just made me feel sick. Reality was that no matter how long I stared at my car nothing would change. My car would still be wrecked. The only solution left for me was to walk back into the school and welcome the change in scenery. Efforts were being made over the loudspeaker to locate the owner of the car parked in front of mine. No one responded, so we assumed that the car didn't belong to any staff member.

CHAPTER 15

Gossip concerning the accident reached me before I left the building. As usual, the grapevine was exceptionally busy. The word was that the entire fiasco was a car chase that went extremely wrong. My car was parked in the last space at the end of the block. Behind me were two stop signs. One was for traffic moving east and the other was for the traffic traveling west. Cross traffic going north and south had the right-of-way. The young man I saw in the handcuffs was a thirteen-year-old car thief driving a stolen Cadillac. At some point the police spotted him and thus began the chase.

Speeds were up to 80 miles per hour in a 25 to 35 mile per hour zone. Eye witnesses stated that he sped through the stop sign at the corner behind my car and was hit by a car from the cross traffic. Knocked out of control, the car he was driving headed for my Chevy. His excessive speed propelled him up the rear of my car, as if it were a ramp, onto the top. His vehicle then jumped off the roof of my car and onto my hood. Most witnesses thought that he probably still had his foot on the accelerator in order to perform those maneuvers. They also believed that this theory would account for what happened next. His car then careened onto the roof of the car in front of mine, but not before turning upside down prior to landing, hence crushing both cars like tin cans. It was reported that the young man jumped out of the car and tried to escape. Would you believe that all he received from his escapade was a bloody nose? If you saw the wreck, you would have thought that there were no survivors. I had never seen anything like this before. Nobody had! The results were that my car was totaled. It was an older car so I didn't carry any collision insurance on it. It was my bad luck that the owners of the stolen car had reported it missing before the accident. Consequently, they could not be held liable for anything that happened after the report was made. This meant their insurance company would not even consider fixing my car. The woman in the car that hit him was not as fortunate as the young man. She was badly hurt and taken to the hospital unconscious and in serious condition. Her car looked like an accordion. Her entire front was almost pushed into the back seat. Everyone said that her wounds were so severe that she might not live. I sincerely hoped that they were all wrong.

It felt like ages but it was only an hour ago that I was speaking to Mr. Johnson; both of us reflected on the calm atmosphere that seemed to be all around us. Within a matter of seconds my tranquil world was shattered. Now I was without a car. We never found out who owned the car parked in front of my auto. The next morning the vehicle was gone. No one knew who took it or where it went. We also heard that the lady in the accident did not survive. Because this young man wanted to have some fun, his antics caused a great deal of grief in many lives . . . including his own. The signs were all there! I'm sure that you could guess that this would not be a Merry Christmas for me.

CHAPTER 16

Teasing can sometimes produce dangerous results. Teasing a gay person can be downright deadly. This is especially true if it's teenagers with volatile personalities, and whose desires and feelings are still in the unfamiliar developmental stage. Joshua Blake was such a person. He was as confused as could be about his sexual preference. He walked and talked like a girl. In addition to that, his body language was more feminine than some women I knew. In school his choice of elective courses were cooking and sewing instead of woodworking or other forms of shop classes. Yet, he insisted that he wasn't gay, and would clearly become extremely angry if he heard anyone refer to him as a faggot or queer. This denial obviously contradicted his lifestyle and his choice of friends. Hanging out with only females in school caused him to be labeled as "one of the girls." Of course, no one would dare utter these words to his face. So due to his explosive temper his classmates always treated him with extreme caution. Until today!

It was two weeks before Christmas, and except for a few minor incidents, the school was fairly quiet. The halls were clear and students were still making an attempt to harness their overzealous temperaments into constructive projects. As I was about to leave my office to attend a Christmas assembly program, five girls almost knocked me down in the doorway. Studying saucer-like eyes on expressive faces, I couldn't help but think that these young ladies would have made excellent models for an Andy Warhol poster.

Breathlessly, they began to yell at me simultaneously, which made it difficult to understand what was being said. I told them to slow down and repeat what they were saying, one person at a time.

Panting noisily, the first student to reach me yelled, "Joshua has gone **crraazy** Mrs. Lawson."

The second girl added,

"He's beating up on Craig something terrible." The third one took over the conversation, finishing the sentence for the others.

"'Cause Craig called Joshua a Tinker Bell, and (*she paused*) Mrs. Lawson, you know what **that** means."

"Tinker Bell?" I repeated. That's a new one on me, I thought, comprehending exactly what she meant.

"Where are they now?" I asked.

"In our class," they all yelled. "Follow us . . . hurry!"

All six of us ran down the hall, turning the corner sharply, and almost knocking Mrs. Harris down. That would have been a tragedy because she was seven months pregnant. Slowing down, I yelled apologies over my shoulder, including explanations of a pending emergency to justify our haste. She waved us yelling, "No harm done." But we could hardly hear her. Practically out of ear range, we increased our speed as we approached the classroom.

The door was closed but that did not obscure the ruckus that could be heard from the hallway. Peeking through the glass window gave me no indication of what was happening inside that room. If I learned nothing else in the six weeks that I was dean, it was to not go barging into an unknown situation. It is important to find out beforehand whether there are any weapons, how many youngsters are involved, and any other relevant factors that could be life threatening. However, this time I had to take a chance and enter without taking precautionary measures.

CHAPTER 17

What a scene! Kids were all over the place. Some were bunched together and close to the ones that were fighting. Others that could not get close to the action were on top of their desks and chairs. My five escorts were sticking to me like glue. I had one attached to each arm and the others were on my heels. Shaking them loose, I waded through the crowd. Getting to the front was a chore. Kids never wanted to give up a good spot when viewing a fight. Loudly yelling the names of students blocking my way gave me extra authority. That always helped in controlling a serious situation. These spectators hated to be recognized at a time like this. It could mean personal involvement when they wanted to remain anonymous. So, they opened a path for me. Damn . . . Another minute and I might have been too late. Joshua had Craig by the throat with his right hand and his left hand was on his leg, trying to hoist him off the floor. Believe me when I tell you that this entire series of events was taking place in front of an open window.

"*Oh Shit,*" I muttered a little too loud, forgetting that there was an entire class present. But I just lost it when I realized Joshua's intention was to throw Craig out that window. Grabbing on to Joshua with both hands, I wrapped my right hand around his neck essentially putting him in a headlock. Then I pulled, and I pulled, and I pulled some more. All the time I was shouting, "Let go of him, Joshua . . . didn't you hear me? I said *let go!*"

I gave it all I had. While all of this was happening, Craig was screaming at the top of his lungs and struggling to keep both of his feet on the floor. However, Joshua wasn't easing up. This uncontrollable teenager was stronger than he looked and very determined to end the dispute his way. Two security guards suddenly rushed into the room. Thank goodness, reinforcements had arrived. It took both security guards and me to drag Joshua away from Craig. Poor Craig collapsed on the floor in front of the window, panting and shaking from his experience. His pants were wet, which meant that he probably emptied his bladder while fighting to keep from falling out the window. A fall from that height would almost certainly have been fatal. Four flights down to the pavement was no joke. After obtaining control of the situation, security had to literally carry Joshua from the room. The entire time he was struggling and screaming threats.

"I'm gonna kick his ass! Let me at him!" he yelled, struggling to break loose from the guards. "Get the fuck off me! Let me go. You better let me go or I'll kick your ass, too!"

His screams could be heard as the security guards dragged him down the hall into the stairwell. The entire time he continued shouting insults until his voice slowly faded away in the distance. Exhausted and upset, I slowly walked back to my office with a very embarrassed and depressed young man at my side. After I spoke to Mrs. Perry, Craig's mom, Janell walked into my room. She had heard about the big fight and was here to lend her support. Passing Craig in my outer office, she turned back to give him a reassuring pat on the shoulder. Janell then peeked into my room to quickly assess my demeanor before she walked in and sat down.

"Are you alright? You have a weird look on your face. Maybe you need to see a doctor."

"I think I'm okay," I said, heaving a sigh as I spoke. "I'll tell you one thing, though, when I get home, I'm going to have a great big glass of wine. My nerves are about to take off and orbit to one of those far away moons in outer space. You know, I thought I was going to end up going out that window with both of those boys. I couldn't get Joshua to release his hold on Craig, and I didn't have enough strength to pull both of them away from the window. For crying out loud, that boy was *stronger* than an ox. I really thought I was a goner. But the worst part was I was on my own trying to save that young man's life. And furthermore, someone needs to give me a good reason why that window was open in the middle of winter. What a miserable day!"

Janell and I talked for about another fifteen minutes, at least long enough for her to believe that I was not going to keel over and pass out at her feet. She seemed satisfied when I said I felt hungry. With all the commotion, I forgot to have lunch. My friend finally left my office taking Craig with her. We agreed that after I spoke to his mother, her next stop would be to speak to Janell. Thank goodness there were no children in my outer office. This break afforded me the opportunity to lean back in my chair and pay attention to my feelings. Closing my eyes I became acutely aware of what was facing me. It was impossible to ignore my head that was pounding from the onslaught of a sudden headache.

CHAPTER 18

It never ceases to amaze me how students could just stand idly by and watch an altercation between friends and never try to stop the violence. Sometimes they even heightened the problem by being aggressive against the adult that is trying to intervene. Our school can easily document that type of behavior from the Halloween fight. Today's dispute was even more troubling because the class was willing to allow a murder to take place while they just stood and watched. Nor did any student try to assist me as I struggled to stop Joshua from accomplishing his disastrous plan. It gives me chills to think about what would have happened if I hadn't arrived at that moment. Craig would have been a goner. Joshua was definitely super charged, so Craig wouldn't have been able to resist his physical attack much longer. Doctors document that at a time like this, the aggressor's anger gives him the strength of more than one person. Joshua undeniably had a high energy level that day. It took three of us to handle him. Now, that brings to the forefront a terrible thought . . . I wonder how long I would have been able to hang on if security had arrived any later to assist me.

In hindsight, maybe this whole problem could have been avoided if Mrs. McDougal, the regular teacher, had not been absent or the substitute had not been late getting to class. She was not familiar with the school and was lost in another wing of the building. Unfortunately, she reached the class after the fight had started. She certainly wasn't able to do anything physical to stop them. Standing

4'11" tall and weighing all of 100 lbs soaking wet, she was no bigger than a minute. Also, it was a known fact that kids always enjoyed giving subs a hard time. I'm sure Craig wouldn't have started this mess with Joshua if their regular teacher was present. Neither Mrs. Bentley, the substitute, nor the students in the class could tell me who was responsible for that open window. Maybe Joshua opened it before the incident in anticipation of his future plans. Who knew? I guess I never would.

The next morning Joshua's mother appeared at my office to fill me in on what happened after the police took him out of the school. I was pleased to hear that he was taken for observation to a psych ward. She apologized for Joshua's bad behavior and wanted me to know that she was transferring him out of the school. I agreed with her decision. According to the rules, he wasn't supposed to return to our school after such a serious problem, anyway. His grandmother, who lived in another state, was going to keep him for a while. Maybe with a fresh start he might be able to find himself. Before she left, I casually interjected a discussion about her son's sexual preference into the conversation. Mom was apparently just as confused as we were about what her son wanted people to believe. I told her to call me if she had any problems getting him settled in his new school. Thanking me, she shook my hand and departed.

Craig's mother also discharged him from our school. I found out that his mother never bothered to even speak to any school staff concerning the incident. She just came in the next day and demanded a transfer. The office staff didn't object, and respectfully honored her request. I guess I can't blame her, either. If it were my child, I know I would have made the same decision. Without a doubt, if Craig had remained at Bradley, he would have a lot of embarrassment to overcome. It would also be a constant reminder that his big mouth almost cost him his life. Recalling what the young ladies who came for my help had told me made me reflect on how deeply words can hurt. Who would have thought that being referred to as "Tinker Bell" would cause a child to take a mental dive off the deep end. All I can do is hope that the students learned a valuable lesson from this horrible display of uncontrollable anger.

There was also a lesson for the adults to learn from all of this. After a lengthy discussion during a faculty conference, we all realized that there could be another explanation for Joshua's lady like behavior. Every once in a while, we might come in contact with a man who likes to get in touch with his feminine side by spending a great deal of time and money on his appearance and standard of living. This type of person would lavish himself in such pleasures as bubble baths, manicures, pedicures and even silk underwear. His clothes would be from the finest stores and made of the best quality materials. Fine dining is a *"must"* with this gentleman and you would rarely see him in a fast-food restaurant. Of course, this man would usually have a good job with a nice salary to finance this expensive lifestyle. Many are successfully married with children and a loving spouse. These men are called metrosexuals and are usually misunderstood and sometimes face a lifetime of ridicule, often being referred to as gay. Since Joshua insisted that he was not gay, maybe we all should reserve our opinions and give him the benefit of the doubt by not judging him. Even if he is gay, that would be his sexual preference and nobody's business. A revised adage made up to fit the occasion came to mind as I sat in my office reviewing the day's events.

"Be careful about what you say about others, because your own words could come back and bite you in your rear."

CHAPTER 19

Three more days before the Christmas vacation! I could hardly wait. They say that time flies when you're having fun. Don't you believe it! Time was flying but there wasn't any fun anywhere. Maybe it was because of my own attitude. Remember? My car was destroyed . . . demolished . . . *gone*! Now I had to either depend on my husband to drive me around or I could take his car when it was available, which was rare. My other means of transportation was by bus. You can believe me when I say I was not a happy camper! All of these inconveniences were definitely more trouble than I wanted to deal with.

On a lighter note, the weather was cooperating with the season. Snow had been falling since early morning. It was now 10:30 and the flakes were accumulating nicely on the cars and sidewalk. Nothing is prettier than fresh falling snow before the human and animal elements leave their mark. I looked out my office window and wondered whether the white stuff was going to stick around long enough to give us a white Christmas. Just like most people who lived in cold climates, I *loved* white Christmases.

Movement in the halls told me the students were on their way to the auditorium. I had forgotten that there was a concert being performed by students made up of representatives from each grade to celebrate the holiday season. The show was entitled "A Medley of Christmas Joy." Even Mr. Ballentine was feeling the holiday spirit.

Surprising everyone, he arranged for Christmas carols to be piped into the students' cafeteria via the school's public address system.

Feeling a little lazy, I rode the elevator to the first floor instead of using the stairs. As the door slowly opened, pure bedlam was taking place right in front of me. Students were running everywhere! Most of the girls were screaming like their lives depended on breaking the sound barrier with their mouths. Not having any indication as to what was causing the young ladies to go berserk, I cautiously stuck my head out of the elevator. Still clueless as to what was happening, I foolishly let the rest of my body follow my head. Did I say foolish? Let me alter that remark to "dumb." Of course, I was immediately hit in the back with a very hard object.

"Ouch, that hurts," I yelled turning to see who or what had hit me.

Instantly, I had to duck to avoid being hit again. Now, it takes a great deal to shock me, but what my eyes saw was even too much for me to absorb. A full-scale snowball fight had developed in the building, and I seemed to have stepped right into the nucleus of the strike zone. Snow was everywhere! Diving into the melee, I helped Action Jackson, and the security guards round up the offenders. A few tried to hide their faces with hoods and coats while attempting to escape, but we caught them anyway. Turning to Action, I sarcastically remarked,

"The custodians are going to love this!" He laughed and replied with an equally facetious answer, "You've got that right! Maybe wearing ice-skates during the cleanup will ease the pain."

Action and I later heard that my perceptive remark about the custodians was on the money. They filed a grievance against the school and requested additional funds to compensate for the devastation as well as overtime to clean up the mess. They contended that this work was far beyond the duties of a normal day's labor. Personally, I felt the kids should be made to do the cleanup. But that was not my call. Also, it was rumored about something in the union rules that prevented non-union participation. Others said it was because it would be child abuse to make them do the work. Whatever the reason, it was left up to the custodians to handle the problem.

You should have seen the halls! The floors, walls, ceiling, and anything else that was in the path of the snowballs were covered with the fluffy white stuff. The auditorium was much worse. In this room the chairs and stage were also affected along with all other parts of the room. How did these kids manage to get so much snow into the school without being detected? I didn't have to wait long for an answer. One of the offenders, James Booker, agreed to talk in hopes of a lighter punishment. He was being held in Action's office. Convincing myself that I wouldn't be satisfied if I didn't hear the saga directly from the "horse's mouth," I hurriedly went to his room getting there just in time to hear James' non-edited version from the beginning.

"Early this morning after the snow had been coming down for a few hours we gathered in the schoolyard with large boxes. Last week it was agreed by all the boys in my class, that we would do this when we got the first snow. We made the snowballs and filled up twenty boxes. Then we hid the boxes behind the four dumpsters out back. Right before the bell rang to change classes, Jimmy opened the back door so that we could sneak our stash into the auditorium. Our plan was that if anyone came into the room we would smack them with snow. Some of us were standing at the door so that we could get the kids not coming to the auditorium. That's how you got hit Mrs. Lawson. We didn't mean to jump you. We thought you were one of us. I guess we made a big mess in the school, huh." My tone was sharp as I responded,

"Oh yeah, you certainly made a big mess; and you're also in big trouble for causing it."

"I guess you're right, Mrs. Lawson. My mom's gonna kill me."

I was happy to hear that. His remorse seemed real and in my position as dean, this was something that I rarely saw from troublemakers. I don't think he was as hard core as the other boys we caught. Maybe he got overly excited about the first snow and fell prey to whatever tales the other boys were dishing out. Even if that was the case, he still had to be punished. I felt sorry for James and really hated to add to his misery. Walking out of Action's office with a five-day suspension in his hand, his drooping head exhibited the emotions of a very sad young man. Adding to his depression was hearing Mr. Ballentine's voice announcing the following message over the PA system. "Due to the antics of a few inconsiderate students, I'm cancelling today's Christmas program and all other holiday festivities."

CHAPTER 20

The Christmas season had come and gone. Entering Bradley this morning made me acutely aware that my vacation was definitely too short. It was the first day back after the Christmas holiday; a group of us gathered by the time clock enjoying stories of vacation escapades and reminiscing about the past ten days. Reliving the past week's fun-filled events somewhat helped to soften the reality of being back. Usually, these periods of togetherness can facilitate putting us in the right frame of mind. Little did I know that the happy feeling I had from the holiday hiatus would soon be a distant memory.

Walking slowly to my office, I stopped periodically to speak to students as they hurried to their classes. As I sat at my desk, I closed my eyes and made a wish that January would be the beginning of a calmer and more relaxing year. You would think that by now I would know better than to believe that wishing would, in fact, work.

The day was progressing nicely, though. Lunchtime passed without a hitch. I was beginning to gradually relax and feel a little complacent due to the peaceful atmosphere that reigned over the school. Dismissal time was only fifty minutes away. I stood at my office door and looked up and down the hall. Not much was happening. Only a few students were passing, and I had a sick young man in my outer office that was waiting to be picked up by his mother. Looking down the hall once again, I saw three girls racing in my direction.

"Now what?" Their faces told me that something was going on. As they approached, out of breath, they exclaimed in unison,

"Mrs. Lawson, come quickly." All three girls were gasping for air as they ran, sporadically stopping to bend over to hold their stomachs.

"Girls, girls, girls . . . stop running! You're exhausted to the point that you can't even talk," I yelled.

Without responding one of the girls grabbed my hand and tried to pull me out the door. The others followed her lead and grabbed my other hand, also in a pulling motion.

"Come! Come!" That's all they would say.

"Wait a minute! What is the big emergency?" I continued to question their motives for trying to pull me down the hall. When they realized that I wasn't budging until they gave me some answers, one of them finally found her voice.

"Your friend is in trouble! Mrs. St. Patrick is trying to get some boys who don't belong here out the building. But they won't leave."

Now, they got my attention! I was just about to follow them downstairs when they revealed the best part of the story.

"Those boys have two pit bull dogs with them, Mrs. Lawson. They turned them loose on the first floor and the dogs are chasing everybody. Your friend needs your help to get those boys and the dogs out of the building."

"Creeps," I yelled backing up into my office. My three young students were steadily looking at me with a "*what's the matter with you*" look in their eyes.

What they did not know was that I had a tremendous fear of dogs, especially unleashed dogs that seem to always approach people who are not dog friendly. In my case, dogs could smell my fear from miles away and took pleasure in running up to me as I looked for an escape route. However, pit bulls were in a class of their own. Experts say that breed could take a chunk out of you if it didn't like the color you were wearing. Something about an enzyme they have that other dogs don't possess as well as the unusual construction of the jaw which allows them to lock on to their victims with a hold that is hard to break. Their fang-like gripping teeth and aggressive attitudes that loudly screamed "*I'm bad*" commanded total respect from all living things, including me. I noticed that the three girls were still watching my expression and I guess it told them everything they needed to know.

"You scared of dogs, Mrs. Lawson? If you are, you better stay here cause you could be hurt badly if those dogs know you scared. You know, they say dogs can smell that kind of thing on people."

I didn't have to be reminded about "what they say about dogs" twice. I plopped down in my chair and told them that they were 100% correct when they said I was fearful of dogs. I recommended that they remained with me, but they wanted to join their class. So, I allowed them to leave.

CHAPTER 21

Where were the security guards? I blamed them for causing me to feel guilty about not doing my part to assist my colleagues. I wondered how everyone was doing against those dogs. Usually, anytime there was trouble with parents or children, I was always there to help. Even before I became dean, I would assist a staff member in need. But this was different. I felt remorseful about my cowardly decision, but against pit bulls, my colleagues would have to travel this trip solo. I'd rather take on King Kong than to come face to face with one pit bull, never mind two.

    I could hear the commotion all the way up to my fourth-floor office. Dogs barking and people yelling were causing quite a ruckus on the first floor. After a while, I felt that the noise appeared to be subsiding. For what seemed like a lifetime I continued to sit motionless in my office. An abrupt knock on the door scared me into such a panicky mess that all common sense went out the window. Now, my imagination had me stupidly believing that those dogs could smell my fear and had found their way up to the fourth floor. A second knock caused me to almost jump over my desk, until it finally hit me that I was being ridiculous. Dogs can't knock! Slowly I opened the door making sure I left room for my eyes only. It was the mother of the sick child sitting in my outer office. In all the excitement, I had forgotten that he was there. I had to open the door for her because I had locked it. Locking the door was just as ridiculous as jumping from hearing a knock at the door, as if a pit bull could knock, or even more absurd . . . turn the knob and walk in. The mother came in and I immediately noticed that she had a really loud voice that was heavily influenced by a striking West Indian accent. To my surprise, she turned out to be a great source of information.

"Girrrl," she said dramatically with her hand over her heart, "you should 'ave been downstairs twenty minutes ago. It was better dan going to da movies. I was in da office getting a pass to come up 'ere when two yoots wit two pit bulls came in tru da door wanting to make mischief. One of dem 'oodlums was yelling to da top of 'is voice 'bout wanting 'is fuckin' coat and not leaving dis fuckin' place witout it. 'Scuse me for using dem dere words to you but, dat is wat 'e said."

She then turned to her son and told him that if he ever used words like that he would be looking for a new set of teeth. In my opinion she appeared to be at ease using those words in front of him. Therefore, I could only assume that her lecture on using curse words was for my benefit, not his. Listening to her speech pattern was intriguing for me. I became mesmerized at the absence of "th" in her pronunciations; and she left off the "h's" at the beginning of words. How unique!

"Anyway," she continued, "I would say 'e must 'ave let 'is girlfriend wear 'is coat to school. It was one of dem leather 8 ball jackets. 'Is woman lef school and came home to tell 'im dat dis bitch in 'er class stole it."

Again, she paused to look at her son and then apologized for the second time before continuing her story. "e went to 'er class looking for da "bitch" wit security "ot on 'im 'eels; and guess wot? Magically, da jacket suddenly reappeared on a chair in da room. Apparently, da girl used 'er smarts and brought it bak. So 'e took 'is jacket and 'is dogs and lef da building. As 'e walked out 'e was yelling dat 'e better never see dat bitch on 'is block. So, Mrs. Lawson, wat do you tink about dat?"

Not wanting to discuss my views with a parent, I thanked her for the information and made an excuse that I was needed elsewhere. She got the message! Saying her goodbyes, she took her son and left.

Classes were being dismissed as I made my way through the thick maze of students down to the third floor. Janell St. Patrick was coming up from the first floor at the same time.

"Where were you last period?" she asked.

The pleasure in her voice told me she was enjoying herself as she waited for my answer. Everyone, including Janell, knew about my fear of dogs. However, she seemed to be overly delighted about my discomfort.

"In my office," I answered trying to keep from having a defensive attitude. Continuing the conversation, I lowered my volume to give it a sympathetic touch.

"I heard about the big problem on the first floor. Sorry I wasn't able to come to your aid. But, as you know, I'm afraid of dogs and Pit Bulls are at the top of my list. Could you please forgive me?"

I included a little pleading tone to add credence to my apology.

"Tell me, are you okay? They didn't bite you, did they?

"No, I'm fine," she said. Luckily, they didn't attack any of us, but they came close. Mr. Ballentine called the police and made out an incident report. They promised to look into the situation. Anyway, who told you about it?"

"Three students and a parent told me everything. But I still would have known something was going on because I could hear the noise all the way up to my floor. Tell me," I asked, "What is so special about that jacket?"

"Well, it has an eight-ball design on the back that is an exact replica of the eight ball on a pool table. These jackets cost a lot of money. I heard somewhere in the three-to-four-hundred-dollar range. Believe it or not, in this neighborhood it is considered a status symbol to own one of these jackets. It can also be a death warrant for the person wearing one. To put it bluntly, some people would think nothing about killing you and then steal it off of your dead body. It is upsetting to know that most kids and their parents don't think about the dangers involved in following this expensive trend. I'm sure the girl that stole that jacket had no idea that her classmate had such a bad attitude boyfriend. You know, he was making a strong statement that was directed at her safety when he turned those pit bulls loose. Fortunately, she got the message. I'm sure you heard that he miraculously left the school with his jacket after he used the dogs to emphasize his demands."

Janell enlightened me for a few more minutes on what happened on the first floor. Most of what she said I had already heard from the parent. Thanking Janell for the fashion update, I left the school that day feeling a little luckier and thankful for not having to confront one of my greatest fears.

CHAPTER 22

A few weeks had passed after the incident involving the pit bulls. Then our school was thrown into tumultuous circumstances again. Only this time the intruders were human pit bulls. A big fight erupted between two mothers outside of the students' cafeteria. At the time I wasn't aware of what the brouhaha was about, but usually when two women tangle, it's generally over a man. Afterward, the scandal around the school was that the boyfriend of one of the mothers was fooling around with the other mother. Apparently, he was seen by a third party coming out of his second lover's house during the wee hours of the morning. This was reported back to his first lover by the lady who saw him, and who also happened to be her best friend. Of course, both women wanted the entire neighborhood to know about his infidelity and for all to see her enemy receive an "ass" whipping. That's why they probably brought pandemonium to the school. They say both mothers accidentally ran into each other at the school. Somehow, I found that hard to believe. Nevertheless, the public display took place during the third period when both of their daughters (who also happened to be best friends) were having lunch.

When the mothers' dispute started, I was in my office refereeing a disagreement between two seventh grade young men. My phone rang. Annoyed that I was being interrupted at a crucial stage in my mediation, I stopped to answer the phone. It was Janell and the urgency in her voice told me that something serious was happening.

"Betty!" Just by saying my name I could tell that she was out of breath. She must have been running. She continued, "We have a bad fight going on down here between two parents. I was there when it started and almost got creamed by one of the women when I tried to intervene."

"Fighting parents? Where are you?" I asked, trying to make sense of what she was saying by getting more information.

"Don't have time to answer many questions. Just come right away to the students' cafeteria. We need your expertise. You seem to have a rapport with parents that many of us don't have. We're hoping you can talk some sense into these two fools. That is, if they ever stop fighting. Also, we might have another problem. Friends of the fighters are watching, probably waiting for a chance to get their licks in. Please hurry!"

She hung up before I could suggest letting all the available men in the building handle those women. I surely didn't share the confidence that Janell had in my abilities. And I definitely didn't want to get in the middle of a "cat fight" between adult women . . . no indeed! Hanging up the phone I remembered my two youngsters. I turned quickly only to find them waiting patiently for my attention. They obviously overheard parts of my conversation and by their looks were dying to see the action first hand. Knowing I had to leave my office, I left my youngsters with parting words to consider. Escorting them to seats in my outer office I told them . . .

"I expect the two of you to act like gentlemen and sit quietly in my office until I return. If I find that you have done anything else besides sit, even peeked out the door, I will be happy to give you fellows a five-day suspension. Am I making myself crystal clear?"

"Yes Ma'am," they said in unison.

That ought to hold them, I thought as I ran down the stairs, sometimes two steps at a time. I could hear the fighters before I saw them.

"Listen bitch, I will fuck you up again if you don't stay away from my man."

"Your man . . . he's at my house every night. That makes him my man. And, by the way, what do you mean . . . again. You ain't fuck me up this time, nor have you fucked me up any other time, ho."

Wow! No wonder their offspring can't get their act together. Listen to these parents! Naturally, this is why we have such a hard time trying to control their kids' mouths in school. Most of the time fighting students won't even respond to an adult's voice unless we insert a few curse words to emphasize our control. Saying "please sit down" to an angry student might get you nowhere, even if you say it three or four times. Saying "sit your ass in that chair . . . ***NOW,***" usually needs to be said only once. Those words could also stop a fight cold. It's really a shame that we have to go to such lengths to end aggressive actions.

Believe it or not, I heard this part of the fight from the second floor. Once I entered the cafeteria, I was shocked at the scene my eyes witnessed. What a sight! These women were worse than the kids. And all of this was over a man who I'm *positive* wasn't worth it. They should have both gone after *him*. At least then they would have gotten some satisfaction. Instead, they tried to disgrace each other. I'll wager that neither one of these ladies would ever hurt a hair on his head. Standing at a safe distance, I evaluated the damage each woman deposited on the other and as well as on the school property. My views have always been that girls fought dirtier than boys and that it is easier to reason with boys. These ladies didn't disappoint me. In fact, they helped me prove my theory. The cafeteria was a wreck and looked like we had just hosted the HBO Saturday night fights. Our mothers were in neutral corners with their daughters by their sides. I felt sorry for the girls. They were crying and pleading with their mothers to stop embarrassing them in front of their friends. Of course they were ignored. Both ladies continued their nonphysical assaults on each other. I say nonphysical because they were prevented by security from getting closer. However, their mouths were still useful and definitely picking up the slack by working overtime. Every curse word in the book was used.

"Bitch, you better get out of town 'cause if I see you in the neighborhood, I'm gonna kill your ass."

"You and what army? You couldn't kill my ass today and it definitely ain't gonna happen no other time. And because I know you need to take anti-stupid pills everyday, let me help you understand better by repeating what I am saying. I ain't going no place. So, take your best and last shot sweetie, cause I'm here to stay."

"Momma, please stop . . . please, pleeease stop!"

I could hear both girls whispering those words to their mothers. They were still sobbing as they spoke softly. Watching this scene made me feel that the roles between mothers and daughters were reversed. Never have I been present during an altercation where the child acted like the parent. How did these two beautiful young ladies manage to be saddled with two of the rowdiest mothers that I have ever seen in my teaching career? Sadly, it seems like all of their pleading and begging were falling on deaf ears. Both mothers continued their disgusting threats on each other. If I had dared, I would have given both of them mirrors so that they could have seen themselves as everyone else in that cafeteria saw them. But I'm afraid they would have attacked me with whatever they had in their hands, cursed me out, and sent me packing. They were in no frame of mind to have a stranger intervene in their private war. I just don't understand why Janell thought that I could make a difference in these two people's lives. Therefore, with that thought in mind I'm going to play it smart and mind my own business.

Focusing on the battle scars of both mothers, I noticed that both ladies were bleeding from their noses and mouths. I believe one mom had a tooth knocked out that she was holding in her hand, while the other seemed to be nursing a black eye with a wet cloth. They were equally covered with scratches, including their breasts. Both ladies were topless but were engaged in holding pieces of their blouses to try and cover their upper body. Moreover, as in most hair pulling altercations, hair extensions littered the floor. Taking all of these facts into consideration, I would deem this fight a draw. Again, I was reminded of my Halloween experience when two young ladies practically ripped each other apart. At this juncture I took time to scan the cafeteria, taking in everything, including the onlookers. As usual, it appears that we all forgot about the students. No wonder . . . they were as quiet as church mice. I don't think I've ever seen them so well behaved. But their expressions told me what I wanted to know. This lunch crowd loved it! And most found it amusing. Our boys were gawking, maybe even drooling until two male teachers put a halt to the side show and lent the women their jackets. I can see why they didn't want anyone to notice that they were still there. That's because they all wanted to stay until the end. Any noise and someone might have emptied out the cafeteria and sent them to the auditorium. If the staff wasn't so engrossed in those women, the lunchroom personnel would have done just that. Therefore, I performed that task: to assist my colleagues on lunch duty and to empty the cafeteria, sending the students to the auditorium for the last ten minutes of the period.

Soon afterward, the police arrived and were able to accomplish what security could not. They got the fighters up and peacefully walking to the principal's office with their mouths shut. The next stop was jail. I really felt sorry for their children who were still crying as they accompanied their mothers to the precinct. The bell rang and the next group of hungry students entered into a now, tranquil cafeteria.

I said a prayer of thanks, for not having to deal with those two mothers or their friends. Over coffee with a colleague, I was informed that during their battle, it took four men to handle those women. I could see why. Both mothers were visibly heavyweights (approximately 250 lbs.-300 lbs.) You could tell that they didn't miss any meals. Unluckily for our staff, each of the men that participated in breaking up the fight weighed less than the women. My colleagues must have had their hands full. Before dismissal the gossip was that one of the security guards went to the hospital for a tetanus shot. It seems that during the scuffle he obtained quite a nasty bite from one of the mothers. Incredibly, there were no other injuries.

The school was never informed of the final outcome between the mothers. Since I've always had an inquisitive nature, it would have been nice to know which lady ended up the victor, thus receiving the male prize. Chances are they either came to an agreement and one mother decided to drop out of the picture; or the choice was behind door number two which meant both ladies decided to *"kick that player to the curb."* Personally, I am in favor of the second option. But whatever decision became the final settlement, it seemed to bring peace and harmony to the neighborhood and to the halls of Bradley Middle School.

One aspect of my job as dean was to try to mold our youth into productive adults. To help accomplish this goal, we stressed the message that violence only exhibits ignorance and never is the answer to problems. Naturally, we expected full cooperation from parents in fulfilling many of our expectations. So tell me, how could we look forward to our children pursuing our lessons when we couldn't get our parents to see the light?

CHAPTER 23

Yesterday's "Battle of the Mothers" was another deja vu moment. I recalled unpleasant memories of a similar incident that occurred within the second month of my appointment to the dean's position. It was just another unfortunate and dumb situation where two ignorant parents felt they had to publicly display their aggressions towards one another.

It started with two students having a fight. Of course, student conflicts happened all the time and most parents took these incidents in stride. But when the mother of the loser snuck up on the child that her daughter fought and smacked her across the face so hard that her nose bled, a small situation escalated into a huge dilemma.

The injured child's mother sought revenge. She came up to school looking for the woman who had the audacity to put her hands on her "precious daughter." Those were her exact words, not mine. Since neither family resided in our school, we all wondered why she didn't go to her opponent's neighborhood to look for her. Somehow, those women felt our school was their own private property to do with as they liked. Mrs. Jennings stormed the school like a category five hurricane accompanied by three girlfriends whose mission was to help her carry out her vengeful deeds. But before she became calm enough to be able to communicate sensibly, we had to be first subjected to her terrible ranting. Her voice could be heard all over the first floor.

"Where is that bitch. She's got an ass kicking coming her way. Who the fuck she thinks she is putting her shitty hands on my baby?"

Let me say that people never ceased to amaze me? I couldn't for the life of me figure out what made her think that the person she was looking for was still in the building. Coming here with her three angry sidekicks was sufficient exposure to make a powerful statement, if that was her intention. She didn't need to have her big mouth get into the act, too. Of course, they knew that this rowdy scene would get back to her opponent. Oh oh . . . her mouth was at it again.

"Whenever that piece of shit shows up, I want y'all to tell her that Maizie's mom wants to kick her ass. I want to know what is her fuckin' problem. What she needs is for me to show her how her ass can get back a double dose of the shit that she dished out."

The teachers' cafeteria is next to the main entrance of the school. A group of us were in the cafeteria on a fifteen-minute break, close enough to overhear her entire trashy speech. I was quite satisfied to remain in my chair and listen to what was being said a few yards from our door without becoming involved. We could hear every screaming word that came out of her mouth from the minute she entered the school; so there was no need to get any closer to the action. But my nosey colleagues wanted to see the face that was attached to the threatening voice.

"Come on, Betty, let's see who's pissed off this time."

That was Ginger Baldwin the art teacher speaking, who never saw any action from her room which was located at the far end of the building. Most of the time it was all over by the time the news of any disputes reached her ears. Since Ginger taught courses that most students wanted, she rarely had problems with her pupils. Her lessons included hands-on assignments like drawing, painting, and even sculpturing. Students were begging to enroll in her classes. And once they were accepted, they didn't do anything stupid to get thrown out. Being ostracized from art might mean ending up with double gym classes as punishment. Nobody wanted that.

So, as you can see, Ginger had it made! But it also meant that she was "out of the loop" when it came to school gossip and excitement. I, on the other hand, saw more than my share of disputes. Being a dean gave me inside information on most of the school's problems. This situation was no exception. I had heard about the mother smacking the teenager and instantly knew that more trouble would follow. What I didn't know was when or how, but I felt that the school might be involved in putting an end to this episode. I wasn't wrong in my assumption; for using this building now gave us the where.

Getting up slowly, I followed Ginger and two other colleagues into the hallway. As fate would have it, we were just in time to witness the two parents grabbing each other by their coats. It was later established that someone eager to see a fight made a few calls notifying the other mother that Mrs. Jennings was at the school mouthing off and looking for her. She obliged her by charging back to the school with her posse, also three friends. This promised to be a good fight and I wanted no part of it. Separating adults was not part of my job description. So far, only the two mothers were fighting while their friends watched. Each side made sure that the main event was not interrupted. I had no problems with that. A few of my colleagues looked my way as if they felt my position gave me jurisdiction over adults. Glaring back at them I silently mouthed the words,

"You've got to be crazy! No way am I getting into that!"

Finally! A policewoman appeared in the doorway with four burly cops. Great . . . reinforcements had arrived! I couldn't imagine anyone in the school capable of breaking up that mess, not even our own security guards. Honestly, all five police were huge and appeared to be handpicked for this assignment, including the female. The chief must have felt they needed the police department's most powerful officers to control this latest incident at Bradley. It worked! Police presence has a way of defusing a volatile situation and this dispute was no exception. The fighting mothers quickly controlled their emotions so that they could escape a night in jail. Smart move! I watched each side assist their friend in picking up pieces of clothing . . . a blouse here and bra there. One mother lost her shoe while the other was missing an earring. What fools! Here we have grown women acting worse than their children. I hoped they realized that nothing was accomplished except torn clothes, lost items, and their self-respect.

Disappointed, my colleagues returned to the cafeteria. Break time was over and they didn't get to see two women battle it out to the finish. Go figure! They were teachers and were supposed to keep the peace. But instead, they were looking to gain enjoyment through someone else's misery.

An anonymous person had called the news media. Lucky for us by the time they arrived, it was all over and everyone was gone. That was all we needed . . . to be seen on T.V. as the feature story on the 6:00 o'clock news. I could hear my neighbors now . . .

"I see your school supplied the entertainment for the night or, you guys need to charge the news media for the great footage they shot on that woman's breast."

My neighbors, relatives and friends knew that my school was located in what some people referred to as a war zone or otherwise known as the ghetto. As a result, from time to time they expect to hear exciting news or information about this neighborhood. And every time the community surrounding the school appeared in the newspaper or a victim was named, I would hear the same questions . . .

"Did you know that person?" or "Is that kid one of your students?"

I guess people felt that I was supposed to know everyone that lived in that area.

Reliving that eventful day had caused me to chuckle at how close our school and the people in the neighborhood came to becoming infamous celebrities.

CHAPTER 24

What a month! The frigid January days were almost over but heated community fireworks seemed to be on the rise.

Early one morning a knock on my office door caused me to look up from the paper work I was trying to complete. "Come in," I reluctantly called out. My door swung open revealing a well-groomed lady at the entrance. Not a hair was out of place. I found that to be a difficult feat due to the almost gale like winds gusting outside that day. In any case, my guest definitely did not look like most of the visitors that entered my office on a daily basis. She was elegantly dressed in a mink trimmed black wool coat complimented by sling back high heels. As if that wasn't good enough, her makeup and nails were impeccable. I invited her to come in and have a seat. During her stroll across the floor, I used the opportunity to continue my inspection.

"How may I help you?" I asked shaking her hand as she sat down.

"I'm here to check on my son. I've been hearing rumors that he frequently skips school. I was also told that he was involved with drugs and drug dealers that hang out in this area."

She continued to fill me in on her son, Jimmy, and his neighborhood activities. Nice dress, I thought as she took off her coat exposing a black low-cut V-neck dress with dolman sleeves. It was a rather long dress that matched the length of her coat. The designer enhanced his creation with a split on both sides that displayed, what most men would consider, well-shaped legs.

Again, it occurred to me that this was not my typical parent sitting on the opposite side of my desk.

She seemed surprised to find out that I'd never met her son. However, I told her that even though we'd never met, I had heard about him. This bit of information seemed to satisfy her.

"I'll send for Jimmy and maybe he can enlighten us on the validity of these rumors."

"I'll appreciate any help you can give me," she replied. "I don't want to go to the police, but he might not leave me any choice."

As we continued to talk, I found out that Jimmy was a sixth grader who just celebrated his twelfth birthday three weeks ago. My goodness, I thought, he's still a baby. It was difficult for me to comprehend that he might be participating in all of these illegal acts at such a young age. I phoned security and requested that they retrieve Jimmy from his second period class and escort him to my office. Since I had the feeling that he was a very slippery character, I didn't want to tempt him into taking a lengthy detour. We didn't have long to wait before I was informed that he was not in class and nowhere to be found in the building.

Mrs. Jenkins became infuriated. She paced back and forth all the while discussing her problem child and how she tried very hard to be a good mother. I sat quietly and listened, understanding her need to vent her anger. It was five minutes before the end of the period when the telephone rang again. It was security calling to inform me that Jimmy was spotted inside the school and heading for his class. They wanted to know if I still needed them to intercept him. I told them I would do it and hung up.

After the third period began, Mrs. Jenkins and I went to see Jimmy's teachers. Since this was a middle school, he had many teachers for us to visit. Every teacher had the same complaint. Some said that he wasn't in class long enough to receive a grade. Other complaints were that he came to class when he wanted to and left when he felt like leaving, even if the period was not over. We heard that he never completed his class work and didn't hand in any homework. And all of his teachers said he lacked the incentive to achieve and would most likely be held over in the sixth grade for another year.

His teachers said that they had been trying to contact a parent for some time. Numerous letters were sent home and messages were left on the phone. Today was the first time they received any response. Needless to say, they were all happy to see her. This was definitely not the kind of news a mother wanted to hear. Mrs. Jenkins told them that she never received any notices from the school and it was by accident that she had come here today. She apologized for their inconveniences. She felt that Jimmy must have been screening her calls and the mail, deliberately destroying all contact from his teachers. To make matters worse, even though we went to all of Jimmy's classes, *he still was nowhere to be found.*

We assumed that he must be hiding out somewhere in the building. Jimmy might not be a good student, but his survival techniques were superb. Associating with the criminal elements in this community was a dangerous game. So far, he was still a survivor and remaining that way was going to be the trick. Sooner or later the violent path he chose to walk could catch up with him. I'm sure that his mother was aware of these facts and the unsafe circumstances that surrounded her son.

Anyone could see that she was not handling all of the recent news well. Also, we voiced our fears to each other concerning the negative influences in Jimmy's life. We both hope it was not too late to reverse these destructive life forces.

CHAPTER 25

Our search for Jimmy began on the fourth floor. As we worked our way down, it was clear to me that Mrs. Jenkins was having a more difficult time containing her anger than I had anticipated. She was walking at a fast pace in front of me mumbling to herself and making growling noises. Every once in a while, she would stop at the end of the hall and look around the corners before proceeding to the next area. At the speed she was moving, it didn't take us long to make our way down to the students' cafeteria.

"Jimmy shouldn't be in the cafeteria," I said turning to Mrs. Jenkins. "This is the seventh graders' lunch time and he doesn't eat until next period. But since we're here, let's take a look."

The second we entered the lunchroom I heard a voice yell,

"Yo Mom, whatcha doing here?"

I was beside myself. I had to admit that I was wrong about where he might be. I stared down at the young man seated in front of me, annoyed at seeing him in a place where he didn't belong. But the second shock I received was realizing that he was extremely small in stature. Based on his reputation and what his mother had told me I naturally assumed that he would be big for his age. In fact, I had visions of a boy who was about 5'4" tall and who had some width to his middle. Instead, I was looking at an adolescent whose height had not yet reached five feet and who was as skinny as a pole. What a surprise!

As I studied Jimmy carefully, I observed that he was dressed just as stylish as his mother. He had on designer "everything" right down to his high-priced limited edition Mickey Mouse watch. In addition to his expensive clothes, the big smile he flashed exposed four gold teeth. He had the brightest grin that I had ever seen. It was apparent that Jimmy was the center of attraction in his group.

Surrounded by boys as well as girls, he was kicked back and relaxed, enjoying all of the attention from his fans. Staring at him with his peers reminded me of the Don in the Godfather movies; or better yet because of his size, Napoleon in that famous painting with his hand stuck in his vest. It was evident that he wasn't here to eat, but just to socialize. It was also visible that those drooling girls considered him "cute." I studied Jimmy carefully, scrutinizing his superior attitude towards everyone within listening distance of his voice. The adoration he received in return from his groupies showing acceptance of his cocky attitude and arrogant manner was nauseating to watch and made it impossible for me to warm up to him. Rarely do I form quick opinions on children, especially the ones that are difficult and cause problems in the school. But, I'm going to make an exception for Jimmy. *I didn't like this kid!*

It was plain to see that he was in the habit of using his smile to get his way. I didn't know if it worked on his mother, but it certainly didn't work on me. Realizing his mother had ignored him, Jimmy repeated his question,

"Hey mom, you didn't answer me . . . whatcha doing here, huh?"

"Checking up on your ass," Mrs. Jenkins snapped stepping closer to his table.

Ah hah . . . I tried to contain my joy after seeing Mom wasn't bamboozled by the smile he obviously used as his conquering weapon. I always loved it when a plan came together, particularly when moms are in the starring role. With a sudden movement Mrs. Jenkins further shocked me by yanking Jimmy out of his seat backwards by the hood of his jacket. He quickly jumped to his feet to keep from falling as his chair toppled to the floor. Still holding on to his hood, Mrs. Jenkins guided him out the door and into the hallway. Jimmy went silently to avoid anymore embarrassment. But he was livid at what his mother did to him in front of the entire cafeteria. Everyone could plainly see that a storm was brewing inside of this youngster.

CHAPTER 26

All the way up to the fourth floor, Jimmy and his mother argued. Quietly, I followed behind, observing but not speaking. I couldn't believe my ears! Hearing a twelve-year-old speak to his mother in that fashion was frightening. By the time we reached my floor the tone of the argument had changed. It was no longer a question from Mom concerning his whereabouts and answers from Jimmy about it was none of her damn business. Mom had finally had enough! She came out and told him,

"I'm tired of your shit. I *will kick your ass* if you sass me again." Jimmy matched her fury with his own explosive words:

"It would make my day just to see you try. *Bring it on, old lady!*" You guessed it! Those fighting words were all the motivation Mrs. Jenkins needed to drop her pocketbook, take off her shoes and launch a full attack on her disrespectful son. The scuffle was on!

Mom grabbed Jimmy with both hands and gave him a punch that landed on his arm. Jimmy retaliated with a punch to her side. She continued to hit him and he would hit her back. While they were going at it, I bent over and picked up her pocketbook and her heels. Up and down the hallway, teachers were peeking out their doors, shocked at what they saw. Students were behind their instructors trying to either look around or over their heads. Shorter students were jumping up and down in order to catch a glimpse of the action. A few of my colleagues were trying to get me to put a stop to the spectacle. I, on the other hand, had no problem with the mother and son "discussion" that was taking place. I was from the old school where parents took charge of their children and were expected to discipline them if they got out of line no matter where they were at that time. In those days, a child would *never* think of speaking to his mother the way Jimmy spoke to Mrs. Jenkins, never mind hitting her. Nowadays, kids are allowed to do as they please. In my opinion, this permissive attitude from parents is allowing a generation of kids to develop behavioral issues that can eventually blossom into serious problems if not channeled into another direction. Jimmy definitely needed immediate redirection. Therefore, my idea on this situation was to let them fight as long as Mom was winning. And she was doing fine!

The fact that it was happening in the school might have been a good thing. If she had waited until they got home, there was nobody there to stop it if things got out of hand. Here, she had many people to assist her. The other factor was that Jimmy was being taught a lesson that he *badly* needed. There was a possibility that his outside drug connections might consider this public exposè too much publicity for them to handle and leave him alone. My only concern was that it might be too little too late to save him from himself. Suddenly, Mrs. Jenkins stopped to look around for her belongings. She noticed her bag on my shoulder and shoes in my hand.

"Don't worry," I told her. "I've got your possessions covered. So, if you wish, you may continue your mother and son session."

What I said satisfied her because she immediately turned back and hit him again. By now we had reached Ms. Bonzell's office. Diane Bonzell, an assistant principal on the fourth floor, was watching from her doorway. Not quite sure about what was happening, she cautiously stepped into the hall. As luck would have it, she moved just in time. Mother and son tumbled pass her and onto her desk, knocking some papers to the floor. Putting a stop to the conflict, I grabbed Jimmy by the same hood his mother had used for leverage and pulled him to his feet. It appeared as if he had had enough. He hid behind me and peeked out at his mother. Mrs. Jenkins, on the other hand, was not finished with her "discussion." It took a lot of convincing from me and Ms. Bonzell to stop her from carrying this any further. She was especially displeased when she realized he caused her to break one of her freshly manicured nails. Calming down, she took a seat and discussed the events of the past hour with Ms. Bonzell.

I must admit that I was extremely pleased at the results of this altercation. I couldn't believe what had just happened. Finally, I had a parent who acted like a parent and not as if she was afraid of her own child. Don't get me wrong! I did not advocate violence. And even though I believed this might have been the best course to explore for Jimmy, I was not at all in favor of physical punishment for all children. Each child should be treated as an independent case. Unfortunately, some children just didn't seem to be able to relate to kind words and positive attitudes. In many cases, they were lacking social skills. These kids considered people who acted sympathetically toward positive treatment "soft." All the evidence pointed in the direction of Jimmy being that type of human being. If any child needed a good thrashing, it was that young man. Of course, I felt guilty about my viewpoint on what took place that day, but I must be straightforward and admit that I was elated when he got what he deserved.

I directed Jimmy and his mother to my office after their conference with Ms. Bonzell had ended. From time to time, I would glance at Jimmy to see how he was handling his fall from grace. His body language told me that he was still seething over his public embarrassment. Feeling that this was not over, I called Janell and requested she come to my office. "I'll be right up," she quickly replied, after I filled her in on the recent events. As guidance counselor, this situation now became her problem to work on and find a solution for this troubled family. I gladly delivered this problem into her capable hands.

CHAPTER 27

T. G. I. F . . . Thank God It's February! I couldn't believe I survived this long as dean. No doubt about it, this had not been an easy job. With all the problems I had to handle in the past few months, I could easily see why the school had trouble filling the position. And based on the stress level that was generated by those incidents, it was also obvious why a person would not want to remain as the dean of discipline.

Things might have been looking up for the school, though. The first few days in the month were uneventful. Small talk about the freezing weather was the big topic of the day. While having lunch on February 2nd, I was reminded that today was the day that the ground hog made his annual appearance. Apparently, he came out and saw his shadow. This was supposed to mean that we were going to have more winter. Everyone seemed to be disappointed that there might not be an early spring. I was really surprised that many of my colleagues actually thought that the ground hog was in control of the weather. Anyway, I supposed I should be thankful for the three days of peace, because on the fourth day, *"shit"* happened again.

During my second period hall check, I stumbled upon five boys huddled together on the back staircase. They were so engrossed in what they were doing that no one heard my approaching footsteps. All eyes were staring at something that was evidently of great interest. Naturally their intense concentration on the object aroused my curiosity. So, on my tiptoes, I moved stealthily up to the group and joined the circle. Placing my hands on the shoulders of two boys, I slid into place between the spectators. They never knew I was there because they were too occupied to look up and check out the newcomer.

Fear engulfed me from head to toe as I looked down at the article that captured their interest. It was a gun. *It was a **real** gun.* I dared not move for fear of detection. My brain went into overdrive trying to quickly devise a plan to get me out of this predicament alive. What was I going to do? I couldn't just walk away. If I tried to leave, I would be noticed. My reputation would be totally ruined. The kids would label me as being "soft." Need I say what that would mean? A dean with that title hanging over his or her head was useless in the job. We were supposed to appear as tough as nails; even if it wasn't true. My next option was to suddenly snatch the gun. I didn't dare do that for fear of accidentally causing it to discharge. That really would present a danger, especially if the bullet hit someone in the group. An added ingredient in this horrible situation was that I was very much afraid of fire arms. I never saw a gun close up . . . until now.

What a predicament I got myself into. I would give anything to be somewhere else at this very moment. However, that wasn't going to happen. No matter how I felt, it was imperative that I deal with the problem at hand. Believe it or not, this all occurred within a short period of time. I'd only been standing there for approximately thirty seconds, but it felt like hours. I had to do something fast before they realized there was an unwanted person in their midst. I decided that the direct approach might take them by surprise and give me the edge I needed. Taking a deep breath I firmly said, "Hand me that gun," I said at the same time sticking my hand into the middle of the circle. Great!

I got the reaction that I wanted. Their expressions reflected a multitude of emotions. Fear, surprise, and even anger were written across their faces as all eyes turned in my direction, but no one moved. Serious as this was, I became amused to see that the element of surprise seemed to have restricted their breathing. So, before they could fully recover from my presence, I repeated my request in a louder voice,

"Are you deaf? I told you to hand me that gun!" Again, there was no response from the group.

Understandably, my main concern was with the child holding the gun. All eyes had switched from me to him. He was not complying with my request. In fact, he stood rooted to the spot in total amazement; he was probably wondering how I managed to infiltrate their private party. Now I really went into panic mode. My insides were churning. I became nauseous, felt weak, and just wanted out of there. But I knew that wasn't going to happen until I *got that gun*.

My worries were many. For one, I hoped that the young man with the gun didn't feel the need to show off for his friends. I would definitely be the recipient of his lack of common sense, which would be an assault with a deadly weapon. Secondly, my need to leave was overwhelming. However, a chicken dean was worthless and my name would be tarnished. Besides, there was no guarantee that I would be able to escape from that group without repercussions. Noticing that they were still off balanced, I realized that this might be my last chance to use their confused state to my advantage. I drew on my inner strength and as a last resort went into my nasty act, hoping to reach these youngsters by speaking in a language they understood. This time I put everything into a powerful voice and yelled, "Give me that damn gun, *NOW!*"

I almost stopped breathing. Quickly assessing the attitudes of my companions, I thought I noticed a slight change in their eyes. It looked like my words were beginning to sink in. It was time to increase the pressure. Lowering my voice to a whisper I continued my lecture . . .

"Every moment you cause me to waste will add to the punishment you receive. I will make it so uncomfortable for you,

you'll wish you were never born. Now, I'm not going to ask you one last time. Damn it boy, give me that fuckin' gun!"

Pure shock appeared on all of their faces following the harsh "f" word that spilled out of my mouth. I must admit that I surprised even myself. At this moment, though, all I could do to salvage my feelings was to make a mental note to say an extra prayer at bedtime, and a great big one in church on Sunday. I had never used that word to anyone before. All cursing is bad! On the other hand, the "f" word surpasses "bad" and holds a special place higher up in the repulsive category. My belief is that cursing should be reserved for emergencies. This standoff definitely fit the definition of a crisis. If my aggressive approach worked, then it was worth the embarrassment. It helped that all the kids appeared to know that my remarks were directed towards the gun holder alone. And one by one they began to react to the severity of the situation by showing their displeasure.

"Hey man, you better give it up," one kid said. "Yeah, we don't want no trouble, Ms. Lawson," remarked another member of the group backing him up.

"I'm not going to jail for nobody," the third youngster spoke as he moved away, detaching himself from the group.

The fourth boy said nothing but backed away from the circle, hoping it would help establish his innocence. The leader had lost his associates! By now he realized that he was all alone with a dangerous weapon in his hand. Taking one more look at his deserting friends, he reluctantly gave up his prize. He placed the gun in my hand, all the while explaining that it didn't belong to him and how he found it in the bushes outside his house. I held the weapon between two fingers; and with the gun hand stretched out as far in front of my body as I could get it, I walked the "fearless five" to the principal's office.

Soon after, during a conference, Mr. Ballentine filled me in on what had happened to the boys. Following my departure from his office, he had called the police. Two detectives showed up immediately. They spoke to our students and ascertained that they were not affiliated with any gang. Fortunately for them, they had never been in any trouble, but seeing the police and having to interact with the officers were enough to give them a scare they would never forget. I heard that they were all requesting bathroom visits and one young man unfortunately didn't make it in time. Under different circumstances I might have been amused, but this was no laughing matter. This was serious business. And even though they deserved to have the devil shocked out of them, I couldn't find any humor in their misery. I really felt sorry for them and the feelings they were experiencing, especially the youngster that brought the gun to school. Four boys were released into the custody of their parents. However, the child that had the gun was unable to go home. He and his mother were escorted to the precinct for further questioning.

Our neighborhood precinct called later that day and explained that the young man who found the gun was really telling the truth. He actually found the weapon in the bushes. Ballistics showed that earlier that week that same gun was involved in a drive by shooting where a young lady was killed. Based on an investigation, lots of controversy about other past crimes seemed to surround this gun. I was thankful to know that such a dangerous weapon was off the street. While clocking out that day, a few of my colleagues complimented me on my courageous move. Maybe it did take nerve to do what I did. But I didn't have a choice.

That evening as I relaxed in a nice, warm bubble bath, I had a difficult time pushing the day's events from my mind. By scrutinizing the occurrences that transpired during the past months, I could only come to the momentous conclusion that somehow trouble looked for and always managed to find me. Some of us constantly seemed to be in the wrong place at the wrong time. Apparently, I was one of those people. I made a mental note to do something about changing my karma.

CHAPTER 28

It's a cruel, cruel world! That was an expression adults often articulated from time to time while they attempted to deal with life's harsh lessons. I was reminded of those words when I accidentally stumbled upon a group of boys examining a gun. If that wasn't bad enough, my nervous system was subjected to a second reminder when I was forced to protect one of our students from the wrath of a dangerous female gang.

Today was Valentine's Day. The morning cruised by with few disturbances. I felt positive this was an indication that this was going to be a great day. The approaching evening would hold a number of valentine pleasures for me. Tonight, my husband and I were triple dating with two other couples. A play and dinner were included in the plans. Looking forward to a romantic evening put me in a festive mood. My spirits were soaring, and I did not intend to let anything or anyone dampen my enthusiasm for the night's celebrations. During school hours, policy dictated that students were not to leave the premises at any time before dismissal. Once they were in school, students must be picked up by a parent or designated guardian if leaving prior to the end of the school day. We were aware, however, that this rule from time to time was ignored by some members of the student body. February 14th happened to be one of those days.

It was the middle of the sixth-grade lunch when Kim Bostic ran up to me. You could always tell when a serious matter was at hand with most students. All you had to do was just look at the eyes which typically took on a different appearance from the normal gaze. Staring up at me, Kim's eyes made me think of two door knobs. She was babbling so incoherently that I could not make any sense out of what she was trying to tell me. Also, it didn't help matters that she had a lisp that became more pronounced when excited. She finally was able to say,

"Mith Lawthan, come quick." As she spoke, she was pulling on my arm.

"Pleathe, Mith Lawthan, you gotta come now." Now she was practically yelling and yanking harder on my sweater.

"What's the matter, Kim? I asked." "I would really appreciate it if you would not pull on me like that," I remarked gently pulling my arm from her to reclaim my appendage.

"But Mith Lawthan you don't underthand. My friend, Dale, left the school to go to the thore. Thum bad people in the yard won't let her come back. They have her out-thide with a knife on her. The security guards won't come out to help. They thay she had no bithneth out there."

Usually, I was able to decode Kim's Speech impediment without much trouble. But this last sentence was almost undecipherable. It was something about the guards not helping Dale because she was outside. I agreed with them on that point. Indeed, this was not looking good. However, it was still their job to assist a student in need. Oh boy! I was getting that feeling of wanting to disappear again. Following Kim to the exit that led to the schoolyard, I looked out the door to see if I could get an idea of what was waiting for me outside the building. I saw nothing.

Opening the door slowly, I looked out and perused the territory. At the far end of the yard, I observed a small group of people gathered in a semicircle. I recognized Kim's friend, Dale, as the person in the middle of this small party. Standing next to her was a young man who had a very familiar face. For the moment his name eluded me.

Stepping out from behind the door I slowly walked towards the group. Deliberately I kept my pace slow and even as to give the appearance of confidence. But the relaxed image I was trying to portray was nowhere in the ball park of how I felt. The closer I got to the individuals the more panicky I became. Out here I was all alone and in a predicament that could cause me bodily harm . . . or worse. I knew I was in the same situation as the day I found the boys with the gun. No matter how much I wanted to, *I could not turn back now.* As usual, in these extreme cases, I always second guessed my decisions. Today was no different. I began muttering to myself,

"I must be crazy to come out here from behind safe doors when security, whose job it is to protect, wouldn't even entertain the idea."

This thought brought a smile to my face. Damn, what is wrong with me? I must really be flipping out to be smiling at a time like this. There's certainly nothing funny about what is happening here.

I was now close enough to see that the person I thought was a young man was really a young woman. She was dressed like a man from her short hair cut down to her pointed toe shoes. Obviously, she was making a statement with her appearance, as if I couldn't guess what it was. As I approached, I recognized my masculine looking intruder as none other than Delcy Thompson. What a surprise! Two years ago, Delcy was one of my eighth-grade students. She was a very big girl with a much bigger mouth. I've always felt that her arrogant personality would eventually get her in trouble. Based on what I was witnessing, I was right. In the past, she was not a violent student . . . just a disruptive one. But we still managed to maintain a civil relationship as student and teacher. Now it was apparent that she had graduated to performing criminal activities. Today, she stood before me commanding five rough looking teens to physically restrain a petrified girl against her will. They were quite a motley group.

Dale's back was against a chain fence. On both sides of her were gang members making sure she could not escape. Why aren't these girls in high school? The thought flashed across my mind but I dare not ask. I didn't want to make matters worse by asking inciting questions. Recognizing me, Delcy quickly turned to her followers and amusingly yelled,

"Yo . . . looka here! If it ain't the big, bad school enforcer. What'ssup, Lawson?"

Well, what do you know? She referred to me as big and bad. I was pleased that she remembered my discipline practices. And to give me the title of school enforcer was really a plus. That's a title our difficult kids gave to the tough deans. It meant that they respected those people and knew that we took no shit. Most students made sure they stayed out of our way. Delcy's descriptive use of "in house" terminology informed me that students who no longer attended Bradley Middle School kept up with our news. It seems my reputation was common knowledge throughout the neighborhood. Considering the situation that I was facing at this moment, being considered "tough" could be a good thing. Maybe I should be flattered. Unfortunately, I didn't have time to savor the moment. Snapping back to reality I responded to Delcy's sarcasm firmly,

"What in the hell do you think you're doing?"

I knew I had to begin my dialogue with a powerful attitude. If I didn't, I would lose the battle before it started. My remark did not intimidate her one iota. She came right back with,

"We caught one of your bitches. She ought to know not to be out here by her lonesome . . . you know what I'm saying? I should cut her throat. I would be doing the school a favor. Then no more bitches would break the rules and come out of school. They'd be too scared the same thing would happen to them . . . You know what I'm saying?"

With that last comment she pulled out a switch blade. In a flash she pushed a button and a shiny blade shot out from its hiding place. Damn it, I needed to go to the bathroom, but that would have to wait. It was my turn to speak and without thinking I sharply voiced my opinion,

"You think you're a bad ass because you have a blade, don't you? What happened to the young lady I used to know? Did you trade her in for a jail cell?"

Those were rhetorical questions. I was not looking for an answer. I was just trying to keep her mind off of using that knife. So, for the first time, I took my eyes off of Delcy and looked over at their hostage. Dale's eyes were huge and filled with tears that had begun to roll down her cheeks. Her legs appeared wobbly and she looked like she was about to pass out from fear. She wasn't alone . . . so was I. Problem was, I had to camouflage my apprehensions, or we might not make it out of here in one piece. Time was running out. With nothing to lose, I continued reasoning with my past student.

"By now, Delcy, the police are on their way. You know the school had to have called 911. Tell me, are you that anxious to give up your freedom? That's what jail time means, you know."

The scowl she displayed on her face was all I needed to know that I had reached a sensitive nerve. Her reaction gave me strength to push a little harder. I went on,

"One thing I've never considered you to be was stupid. To harm her in any way would definitely be labeled as a really dumb act."

I paused for my words to sink in. Thank goodness, it looks like she's listening. A hopeful feeling for a successful ending to this standoff had suddenly materialized as a possibility. Taking this as a positive sign, I decided it was time to put an end to this situation one way or another. Lowering my voice, so that only Delcy could hear me, I said,

"Turn her loose before it's too late. Two years ago I saw beyond your rough exterior and realized there was a young lady with a promising future. I still feel you can put this life of crime behind you and become an asset to society. But, if you pursue today's course of action, nothing anyone can say or do will help. *Besides, I will personally make it my business to make sure you go down for this. All the way down."*

This last statement was really a bold threat. I was hoping it would shock her into reality. However, it was also an unintelligent thing to say. I didn't consider the consequences that could follow behind such a remark. It could backfire on me and make matters worse. I was sorry I said it, but it was too late to take it back. Delcy and I stood face to face for a few seconds, neither of us saying a word. It felt like an eternity. Finally, she broke the silence with a loud laugh. Then she yelled to her gang, "Lawson's got balls!" Turning back to me she stated, "I must admit you were my favorite teacher. Do you know why? It's 'cause you ain't scared of nuttin'. I can respect that 'cause I ain't scared of nuttin', either."

Pausing, she gave me a long inquisitive look. Then with a big smile she said, "Okay Lawson, I'm gonnna do you the favor you're asking for. I'm gonna let her go. But you and everybody in that school better make sure I never catch that bitch out here again. In fact, I better not catch any of your bitches. The next time I ain't gonna be so nice."

Delcy turned to her two associates holding Dale and nodded her head. They immediately released their hold on the panicky youngster. Dale ran to me and buried her head in my chest. Her eyes still on me, Delcy flipped her knife closing it with one motion. This whole scene didn't feel real. I felt like I was one of the actors in a second-rate gangster movie. Looking around I realized that we weren't out of the woods yet. The entire gang was watching me. I figured Dale and I better get out of here before Delcy changed her mind. Bending over I whispered to Dale,

"Start walking slowly toward the door and don't look back. Don't worry; I'll be right behind you."

She turned and headed toward the building. Thanking Delcy for her cooperation, I slowly paced my steps behind Dale.

CHAPTER 29

"The Long Mile." That is what I called the distance we walked between Delcy's gang and the school door. In order to get to the building, I had to turn my back on Delcy and her cohorts. I wanted to walk backwards, but I couldn't for obvious reasons. I was taking a big chance because I had no idea whether I was going to be hit in the back by sticks, stones, a knife or even a bullet. I told Dale not to turn around. I know that must have been a difficult task for such a young child to obey. Following behind her, it was almost impossible for me to resist the urge to look back, as well.

After what seemed like forever, we reached the school. What a reception awaited us! We were greeted by the principal, two assistant principals, Action Jackson, security guards, four policemen, and what seemed like half the teaching staff. Now, for the first time, I turned around. Looking out the glass window in the door, I scanned the yard. Delcy and her posse were nowhere to be seen. They probably saw the police cars out front and decided that this was a good time to disappear. I asked Action Jackson to drop Dale off at my office while I kept an important appointment. I told him I would be up there in approximately ten minutes. Taking my leave, I headed for the first-floor bathroom.

When I finally reached my office, I was pleased to see that Dale was still shaken from her recent encounter with the gang. I didn't want her to ever forget what happened in that school yard for a long, long time. As far as I was concerned, today's events were much more frightening than the gun episode on Groundhog Day. I definitely didn't need all this drama in my life.

Picking up the phone I called Dale's mother to inform her of her daughter's narrow escape from the gang. Mrs. Graber treated the news with indifference. She thanked me for rescuing her daughter, but, also gave me a two minute lecture on how she felt I was exaggerating the circumstances surrounding the incident. What a fool. She had a hell of a nerve! She should have been apologetic about her daughter's bad judgment in disobeying school rules. She should also be thankful that someone risked their life to rescue her daughter. Instead, she found it necessary to tactfully call me a liar. Her flippant attitude just made my mood worse. In fact . . . *I was furious!* If I could have jumped through the phone line and punched her in the face, I would have done so without considering the consequences. Yet, I kept my cool and spoke to her in the most patient voice I could muster up.

"Mrs. Graber, it is clear to me that you do not consider this a problem. Therefore, I must inform you that there will be some changes made on how I handle the next gang incident involving your daughter. I will *not* jeopardize my own well-being or the welfare of any other school personnel by repeating today's process. I *will* send for you immediately. That way *you* will be able to have the sole privilege of dealing directly with these people. Maybe with personal contact your definition of an exaggerated event will change."

There was total silence from her end of the phone. You could hear a pin drop. Evidently, she did not receive the response she expected. I decided to break the silence by continuing with a discussion on her daughter's punishment.

"I'm suspending Dale for five days. Please review the school's policies with your daughter during her time at home. When her five days are up, a parent must accompany her when she returns. Let's hope that she comes back with a different attitude, and ready to acknowledge and obey the school's authority. It is important that we all work together for Dale's benefit so that she fully understands what can happen to her when she ignores the rules. *We must make sure that this does not happen again."*

I ended by thanking Mrs. Graber for her cooperation; and before she had a chance to respond, I said goodbye and hung up, abruptly ending the conversation.

Sitting back in my chair I tried to relax by taking several deep breaths. I was still smoldering from Mrs. Graber's nonchalant remarks and "devil may care" attitude. Besides that, I still had not completely calmed down from the school yard episode. At this very moment, I felt like an overstretched rubber band ready to snap. Fatigue was beginning to take over. How long did I have to wait before I could go home? Glancing at my watch I saw that I had one hour and 20 minutes more to go. Anyone that saw me now could instantaneously tell that I probably needed this time to get my emotions under control. I *must* not allow what transpired today to mess up tonight's Valentines celebration. So using this hiatus to my advantage, I laid my throbbing head on the desk, and quietly waited for the bell to ring.

CHAPTER 30

The rest of February breezed by with only a few minor incidents. One occurrence dealt with a gay male student who punched another classmate in the mouth knocking out one of his teeth. This was all because the classmate was laughing at his feminine walk. I might add that dealing with their parents wasn't too pleasant, either. Next, we had two huge female students that got into a scuffle in the auditorium. Both were suspended, mostly because the teacher that tried to intervene was knocked down and ended up in the hospital with a dislocated shoulder.

Then I had to deal with Sean Duncan who was sent to my office because he was as "drunk as a skunk." He was so intoxicated I wondered how he managed to find the school building. I sent for his mother. When she saw how plastered he was, she flew into a rage. When asked for an explanation about her son's condition, Mom made many excuses. But the biggest tale I felt she told me was that she didn't know he had a drinking problem. I found that hard to believe. It was doubtful that this was his first encounter with alcohol. Besides, his inebriated condition was impossible to hide. While Mrs. Duncan was present, I decided to do my own preliminary investigation on his behavior pattern within the past month. What I found out supported my theory. By speaking to some of his classmates I was able to piece together what had been happening to Sean. Students reported that he came to class at least five times in the past month smelling of liquor. They also related that his friends covered for him. That way his teachers weren't aware of his drunken condition. Today in my office he smelled like he fell into a distillery vat. We all could detect the strong scent of beer from across the room. Upon further communications with his classmates, they acknowledged that this was the first time he was drunk enough to stumble. What's more, they all agreed that usually he was able to control his actions much better than what we were observing at this moment. This was an indication that the problem has escalated.

Discussing my findings with his mother, her anger abruptly turned to tears. She honestly seemed unaware of his problems, including the fact that his grades were poor and he was a candidate to be held over. We sat and talked for over an hour. She seemed to need to get a lot off of her mind. Like many moms, Mrs. Duncan was a single parent raising four children. There was no positive male role model in Sean's life. Support for the family came from mom's working two jobs. This did not leave her much time to supervise her children's activities. Reluctantly, she admitted that her kids were by themselves a lot, and she didn't know how they spent their spare time.

It was time to get the guidance counselor involved. I referred her to St. Patrick. Group therapy and counseling were definitely needed to salvage this family. Perhaps Janell could find a way to help Mrs. Duncan spend more time at home without losing any income. On my calendar I wrote myself a reminder to check on Sean and his family in a month to see how they were coming along.

CHAPTER 31

March was true to its temperament. The beginning of the month came roaring in like a lion. The weather for the first half of the month had everybody talking. Heavy rains would soak the area one day and other mornings we would wake up to a cold liquid falling that was mixed with snow. It appeared that winter and spring were having one huge disagreement. Fortunately, life in my educational establishment was bearable. A few insignificant disputes took place, but for the most part the atmosphere was one of serenity.

On March 14th during one of my frequent patrols, I stumbled upon a teacher in tears sitting on the back stairs. Ms. Puryear was a small woman in her mid-fifties. If I were to guess her height and weight, I would say she was approximately four feet nine inches tall and weighed around ninety pounds. Oddly enough my attempt to communicate with her ended up as a one-sided conversation. She would not talk and resisted any attempts I made to elicit what was troubling her. But after much coaxing Ms. Puryear finally spoke and couldn't seem to stop after she got started. In fact, she continued for twenty minutes. Since this was her free period, I let her talk. She chatted about the students and her colleagues and her mother and anything else that was bothering her. However, her immediate problem dealt with a group of eighth grade students.

Puryear had just finished teaching the class that used to be my homeroom. During the period, Jasmine, one of my larger girls, picked Ms. Puryear up and carried her outside of the classroom. Some of the other girls used this opportunity to take money out of her wallet. After they were finished, Jasmine brought Puryear back and deposited her on top of the desk. Today the bell rang ending the period while she was still on top of the desk. Since they would make sure to remove her chair before leaving the room, it was extremely difficult for her to climb down from that height. She said she felt angry and humiliated and could still hear the students' laughter ringing in her ears. She also stated that this was not the first-time students had done embarrassing things to her. These same girls had robbed her twice before; and fear of the students has kept her quiet. In fact, if I had not found her today, this incident would have also gone unreported.

I called the main office and arranged for a teacher to cover her next period class. Then the two of us paid Action Jackson a visit. After hearing the story, Action and I agreed that those kids had to be taught a lesson they would never forget. They had been escaping punishment for all types of illegal shenanigans. And their cocky attitudes were sending the wrong message to their classmates. Bradley had to set the record straight! We started by calling the police. Next, it was imperative that we wait for them to arrive. That way we could make a united entrance into the girls' classroom. Bringing order back to this class would begin with the arrest of Jasmine Jacoby.

Jasmine was taken out in handcuffs. There was no resistance from the youngster; only a look of pure panic. The entire class watched in silence. One student voiced her opinion and probably verbalized the thoughts of others in attendance.

"I can't believe that weasel of a teacher snitched. I didn't think she had the guts."

Unfortunately, they were right. If not for my insistence and speaking up for her, she would not have had the guts. She was afraid of these kids. So, I had a lengthy discussion with them which was more like a scolding supported by a threat. They were told that if anything happened to Ms. Puryear, at any time, they **all** would be arrested. It wouldn't matter who was to blame. Every one of them would be responsible for the assault. I asked them if I had to repeat my statement for them to better understand what I meant. They all nodded no. But at this moment I'm sure they were not thinking about Ms. Puryear. They were thinking about themselves. Listening to the students' whispers convinced me that their biggest concern was Jasmine and whether she was going to tattle and name her accomplices. If she did talk, the question was who was going to be offered up for sacrifice? After all, Puryear never saw the other students that were involved. She was taken out of the room by Jasmine while they did their dirty work. So, only Jasmine could do damage by naming names. This little bit of information made me wonder. Exactly, how many more *were* involved?

That night, as we envisioned, five more students were arrested. It seemed that this conspiracy was bigger than we thought. Some students, which Ms. Puryear didn't know about, were acting as lookouts. Any money that was taken from her was divided between the participants. Jasmine had told all and implicated everybody. What a shame! The news really upset me. Those were my students. I taught them for almost two months. In that short period of time, I had developed a special bond with most of the youngsters. Especially Jasmine! She happened to be one of my favorites. She was a big girl, but she was also a very affectionate child. One day in class I had a coughing spell. Jasmine ran out of class and came back with some water for me. She was concerned and I appreciated her display of kindness. She would have been the last kid in the class that I would think would get into trouble. I can't believe I could have been so wrong.

We lost a good teacher when Ms. Puryear quit. She was concerned that Jasmine's friends might blame her for the arrests and cause her harm. She didn't want to see them again. Nobody could have blamed her. Based on how they had treated her, I would have arrived at the same decision. Therefore, the day of the incident I escorted her to her car at three o'clock and wished her happiness at her next school.

As far as what the future held for Jasmine and her partners, they were processed at the precinct and released into the custody of their parents. This was truly a lucky break for them because Ms. Puryear would not press charges. They could have been sent to a juvenile institution for six months or more to pay for the crimes they committed.

Like other dangerous offenders, these kids were discharged from Bradley Middle School and sent to one of the alternative educational establishments in the area. Their departure was accompanied by a stern warning of possible jail time from the local law enforcement if they were involved in any more criminal activities. I guess the warning worked. No more negative news filtered down to our school about any of those kids again. That was definitely a good thing!

CHAPTER 32

Life is strange! All of a sudden time seemed to be slowly passing by. It was now the middle of March and three more months to the end of the term. Looking back, on Ground Hog Day the news media reported that the little critter saw his shadow and dove back into his hole. So, because of his actions, six more weeks of winter were predicted. In the weeks that ensued, we found out that his predictions were extremely accurate.

The entire staff was talking about the unrelenting freeze that crippled our state. Emergency maintenance vehicles were seen everywhere trying to deal with exploding water pipes, stranded cars, broken heating systems, and other weather-related crisis. The penetrating arctic winds were brutal, thus causing us to endure the coldest temperatures of the entire winter. Those conditions did not make for happy circumstances within the walls of Bradley Middle School. Students were restless and needed to expend some of their negative energies beyond the school walls. The school yard was always their main outlet for venting pent up emotions. However, Mother Nature was not being kind. Along with the deep freeze, weeks of snow accumulation made it impossible for students to use the yard for recreation.

To add to the inconvenience, the inclement weather made it difficult for many staff members to reach the school. Automobiles were rendered useless as they were practically buried by the plows heaping snow against them while clearing the streets. Buses were operating but were a slow means of transportation. When they finally arrived, they were overcrowded with people who pushed their way onto the vehicle even if the only room available was to ride on the steps. Consequently, what was usually a fifteen-minute ride could now take an hour or even more to reach the school. On the other hand there was always walking. But unless you were in excellent condition and had approximately two hours or more to spare, walking was not an option to even consider.

Seventy eight percent of the teaching and administrative staff managed to dig out their cars and drive through the treacherously slippery streets to greet those diehard students that made an effort to come. Some youngsters came because they really wanted an education. Others made an appearance because their parents forced them out into the cold wintry morning. Either way, we only totaled four hundred thirty seven out of fourteen hundred students. For two glorious days of low attendance, peace reigned throughout the quiet halls of Bradley Middle School. You guessed it . . . this lull didn't last long. Four days after the school resumed regular sessions, a feisty new student was introduced to our already hyperactive student body. First impressions were that she was a very small young lady with a docile personality. She seemed very sweet and looked like she wouldn't hurt a fly. However, it didn't take us long to find out that her looks were very deceiving.

It was the beginning of the third period on a cold Friday morning. Today, this hour found me in my office trying to decrease the tremendous mound of out-of-control paperwork on my desk. A loud yell brought me to my feet. What in the world . . . ? The sound seemed muffled and only happened once. Not sure about what I heard but assuming the noise came from the stairs closest to my office, I immediately left to investigate the area.

Cautiously I pushed the door open revealing Mrs. Spellman, a seventh-grade math teacher. She was on her knees with one hand on her head and the other hand holding on to the banister.

"What happened?" I asked guardedly looking around to see if there was an attacker lurking and waiting to attack again. As I helped her to her feet, she breathlessly exclaimed, "I don't know why but some girl ran passed me, punched me in the face and pulled my wig off. My wig is held tight by bobby pins so she also yanked a bunch of my hair out, too."

I inspected her face and noticed a little blood on her lip. She said she was okay but I felt she should receive medical attention. So, during our walk to the infirmary, Mrs. Spellman gave me a description of her attacker. I notified security that a girl in a red sweater attacked a teacher on the fourth floor. I also asked the guard on the phone to notify the other school security plus all available personnel to do a sweep. Sweeps are very effective. The process involves every staircase, including the halls on every floor, to be infiltrated with all available personnel. Teachers with free periods, administrators, custodial staff and all others who are available at the moment, must be on the floor at the same time. There is no place for the hunted to hide, and as a result, students are usually caught in the web. This course of action is excellent for trapping cutters and intruders. Students caught in the ambush are taken to a central location, usually the auditorium. Here we check for classroom passes or written permission to be out of class. Those with passes are allowed to continue to their destination. Those without authorization are escorted to one of the deans for further processing. Intruders are processed by security. If they are first- or second-time offenders they are escorted to the door and sent home with a stern warning. Our tougher guests and constant repeaters are turned over to the police.

Our sweep was a huge success. We caught the girl in the red sweater along with three cutters and two intruders. Security took the intruders, Action Jackson got the three cutters, and as you would expect, I got Miss LaKeisha Rooter.

CHAPTER 33

I found out her name when she sarcastically offered it up along with a nasty attitude. During our discussion I learned that she was a new seventh grader transferred from another school. As I inspected her from head to toe, I estimated her weight to be approximately between ninety and one hundred pounds. For such a small person she sure had a huge attitude problem accompanied by a big mouth. She stood in front of me looking down at the floor, a hand on her hip that jutted out as far as she could push it to the right. She was obviously on the defensive, ready to tackle all hurdles that got in her way. I realized that she considered me one of those hurdles and I was going to have to handle this one differently. Whenever I came face to face with an obstinate student, male or female, I found that addressing them by Miss or Mister sometimes weakens their defenses. So, I began, "Miss Rooter, why did you attack Mrs. Spellman?" My question extracted an overly rambunctious response.

"First of all, I ain't attack nobody. Second, who the hell is Mrs. Spellman?"

I could see she wasn't going to make this easy, so I continued in a quiet voice hoping my attitude would calm her down.

"Mrs. Spellman is the teacher you punched and yanked her hair out." Again, LaKeisha answered in an angry voice.

"I ain't punched no teacher. If a teacher said I did, she's a damn liar. I wasn't even on the fourth floor."

Eureka! She fell into my trap. If you let them talk long enough they'll usually hang themselves. I switched my tactics. My voice became harder and more demanding.

"How did you know that the teacher was assaulted on the fourth floor? I never said where she was. All I asked you was why did you attack her."

LaKeisha's tough shell was beginning to crack. She realized her error too late to retract the statement. However, she was still trying to camouflage the truth with her song and dance routine. She gave her defense one last try. For no reason at all she began to yell at the top of her voice.

"I ain't gonna take no shit from none of y'all. Who the fuck you think y'all is trying to pin this on me? Y'all don't know me. None of y'all don't know who you messing with. I'll kick her ass for real and if you get in my way I'll kick your ass too."

Whoa . . . this little "B" has a hell of a nerve. I couldn't believe my ears heard correctly. Imagine speaking to an adult like that. Back in the old days when I was a youngster, a child wouldn't dare think those degrading thoughts; never mind speak them. Now anything goes with this generation. Children have no respect for themselves or anyone else. Besides, that last remark stung because it was directed at me. I held my temper and kept my sharp tongue in check. Instead of retaliating, I said to her in a voice as slow, and with as much tolerance as possible, "I believe you better rethink those remarks you just made. Unless you plan to spend some time in jail, you're not going to kick anyone's ass. And just to set the record straight, maybe you got away with your nonsense at your other school, but I can personally guarantee you that we won't accept *any* of your mess here."

My head was down filling out a behavior form on her as I spoke. Without looking up I could feel her eyes boring a hole in my head. I was waiting for a response that never came. All she did was stare at me. That's good! Maybe she's finally learning to keep her big mouth shut. Breaking the silence I remarked,

"I hope you realize that you could go to jail for assaulting a teacher. Are you in that much of a hurry to have a record at your young age?"

At this point I stopped writing and looked into her eyes. I wanted to see what reaction the threat of being incarcerated might have on her state of mind. She was just a baby . . . only thirteen years old. I knew that she wouldn't be placed in an adult jail. But I'm not sure she knew that. At least I hoped she didn't. I knew she would end up in a juvenile corrections facility. Honestly, it didn't matter where she ended up; confinement in any of those places was depressing. I could see in her face that she was paying attention even though she tried to pretend that she was occupied with picking and biting her nails.

Using this silence to check on the injured teacher, I contacted the nurse to obtain an update on Mrs. Spellman's condition. She was still under observation for precautionary measures. Mrs. Spellman was a lady in her sixties and the principal was not taking any chances with her health. I relayed this information to LaKeisha. I wanted her to know that her disgusting behavior might have caused serious injuries to another human being. However, before I could finish my lecture I was surprised by her sudden display of remorse. Tears rolled down her cheeks. From what I observed about her personality, this definitely appeared to be out of character. Of course, this new attitude made me wonder. Was this for real? Could she really be concerned for the teacher she attacked or was she bringing on the water works just for my benefit? Then again maybe the answer was a third choice. That would mean she was feeling sorry for herself and the mess she caused and knew that the prognosis for getting her little rear end out of this dilemma wasn't favorable. Whatever the reason, LaKeisha was certainly pouring it on. As her sobbing increased, her small body began to shake. I sat and watched her for a few minutes, not saying anything. Somehow, I felt she didn't cry too often and needed this release. After a few minutes I asked,

"Why are you crying?"

Her response took me by surprise.

"All y'all teachers hate me, my sisters and brothers hate me, and even my mom hates me. Nobody in school wants to be friends with me. But I don't care. I hate all y'all too and I don't give a fuck about what I did to that teacher. She deserved what she got."

CHAPTER 34

I looked at her a long time before I responded. Times like this you don't want to say the wrong thing. God only knows what the correct words would be. Anyway, I was going to try my best to temporarily aid this youngster's troubled mind until I could get her some professional help. Calmly I began to speak,

"LaKeisha, you don't really mean what you just said. I can tell you have some issues that you might have to work on. But anything can be fixed, and I know that everything will be all right."

Then trying not to choke on a little white lie, I smiled at her as the words rolled off my tongue,

"I'm sure your family cares for you and, for that matter, I like you" (*there, I got it out*) "and I would like to help you. In fact, there are a lot of us right here in the school that would like to help you." (*That part was true.*) "But we need something from you in return."

Now I had her undivided attention! She stopped crying and was concentrating on trying to read the expression on my face for answers. I was impressed. It was interesting to watch her powers of deduction struggling to figure out what adults wanted from her. No doubt she considered my face an open book and she possessed the skills to read what was written on the surface. Apparently, she liked what she read because her next words were uttered in a more civil tone.

"What y'all want from me?"

"For starters" I began, "We want you to stop cursing at everyone. Believe me when I tell you that it's not in your best interest to behave like a fool. Sorry for being so blunt but it cuts to the core of what I'm trying to say."

LaKeisha nodded her head in acceptance of my explanation.

"Your type of attitude only turns people away from you and gets you the opposite reaction to what you are seeking. I know that is not what you want . . . is it?"

"No!"

She sadly responded in a low voice as she wiped her nose with her sleeve. I offered her a tissue.

"I'm taking you downstairs to see Ms. St. Patrick. I want you to tell her everything you've told me. But before you speak to her, make sure you lose the attitude. Remember, being nasty won't help you at all."

"Who's Ms. St. Patrick?" Now, all of the attitude was absent from her voice. I responded,

"Ms. St. Patrick is the school's guidance counselor."

Before I could continue what I was saying she asked, "What does she do?"

"Well . . . she takes care of students who have problems and tries to help solve whatever is bothering them."

"Do you think she can help me?"

"Yes, she can. But that also depends on whether you allow her to do her job. That means remaining calm and being cooperative. Do we understand each other?"

She nodded yes.

"So, what do you think? Do you want to try it our way for a change?" Without hesitation LaKeisha nodded her head and said, "Yea, I'll let her do her thing."

"CAUGHT" IN THE MIDDLE

As she spoke, I was dialing Janell's office. I didn't want to give this young lady time to change her mind. Most often Janell is at meetings or in a conference with a parent. However, as luck would have it, Janell was in her office and agreed to see LaKeisha right away. I escorted LaKaisha to the guidance office and after introductions, left them to get acquainted.

A slow walk back to my office gave me the opportunity to think about the events of the past couple of hours. I wondered about what happened in this youngster's life to cause such a negative response to society and anyone else that came in contact with her . . . including her family. Janell had her work cut out for her if she was going to turn this child's life around.

At 3:15 I met up with Janell at the time clock. I asked her how she was getting along with LaKeisha. She smiled and remarked that this student could turn out to be one of her most challenging cases.

"You know that I'm not a quitter," she said in a whispered tone.

"You also know that I will do everything that can be done to help her."

Nodding my head I said, "I know you can do it!"

She was not exaggerating. I would wager a nice bet that Janell would use all of her years of experience and knowledge to solve as much of this youngster's problems as possible. I remembered when we had this case in February with an alcoholic student and his overworked mother.

While keeping up with the progress of this family, I watched Janell work miracles to successfully help Sean Duncan and his family out of an impossible situation. Her first challenge was Sean. She wasted no time in placing him in a program for teenage alcoholics, and arranged for him to stay in a group home while he was going through the drying out period. This immediately took stress out of the house for not only his mother but also his siblings. His younger brothers certainly did not need to be exposed to all of that drinking. On the positive side, it was good that they could see that nothing constructive came from their brother's addiction to alcohol. Next, she helped Mrs. Duncan apply for public assistance. There are many applicants who try to cheat the system and don't really need a helping hand. Mrs. Duncan was not one of those people. She qualified for all the assistance she could get. With Janell's help she was able to quit her second job and received financial aid to assist with the money that she was lacking. Mrs. Duncan was so grateful for all the support she received; she baked Janell the most delicious cake I had ever tasted. That was unquestionably a successful case.

Hoping to have the same success with LaKeisha, Janell and I went to see Mrs. Spellman, detaining her as she was about to leave the nurse's office. After speaking with the teacher, Janell and I agreed to honor her recommendation to not suspend LaKeisha. We all decided that it would not serve any purpose to add a five-day absence to her already problematic case. And it could moreover hurt any progress that was made in today's counseling session. Before we took our leave, we questioned her on her injuries and how she was feeling. She assured us that she was doing much better and with a little rest would be fine. I felt guilty for not suspending LaKeisha for her nasty attack, but when I heard Mrs. Spellman's self-diagnosis of not being seriously injured, it somewhat helped to ease my conscious. After leaving Mrs. Spellman my colleague and I continued to discuss the case, offering up theories on the kind of home life LaKeisha might have. Based on all those details, and in conjunction with our obvious lack of knowledge on the type of situation we were dealing with, we opted not to make any hasty decisions that could cause more traumas in this teenager's life. We also agreed that it might be best if Janell were to tactfully talk to her mother in order to ascertain exactly what was going on inside of that home to make this youngster feel so unwanted.

"Good Luck," I yelled over my shoulder as I walked out the door. However, like some of the other cases I was involved with, I couldn't shake the uneasy feeling that we hadn't heard the last of LaKeisha Rooter, especially if we were not successful in getting to the bottom of her family differences. Past experiences with other troubled students had educated me to know that future occurrences with Ms. LaKeisha might not be pretty.

CHAPTER 35

News travels fast in some middle schools. Our school was definitely known for an extremely rapid communications highway. Deans relied on sharp teachers with keen sight and hearing to intercept pertinent information from this highway as it moved swiftly among the student body. Some students felt these teachers were always sticking their noses where they didn't belong. This was a good thing, especially since a sharp-eyed teacher with good hearing and a nose for trouble probably stopped a catastrophe by alerting us to an overheard conversation among four boys.

It was a gorgeous Tuesday morning during the first week in April. Instead of holding the students in the auditorium, the principal decided to have morning lineup in the school yard. Students and teachers gathered in small groups to talk while waiting for the bell to ring. Mrs. Pierce, a sixth-grade teacher, didn't attach herself to any group. She was like me . . . a roamer. There were a few of us that utilized our time leisurely strolling through the yard meandering among the students. We might stop occasionally to say a few words to a student or exchange greetings with a colleague. But, for the most part, we continued on a constant path always with a watchful eye for sudden problems. On this particular day, Mrs. Pierce noticed three of our students in deep conversation with a youngster who did not belong on the premises. She recognized the child as a former student of ours who had attended Bradley two years ago. It so happened that all four kids were well-known by the staff. Of course, the main reason for their popularity was their growing jail records. But our visitor had the worst reputation of the bunch. He had been arrested several times within the past year. One time in particular was for armed robbery. Mrs. Pierce got my attention with her eyes. She rolled them in the boys' direction as a signal to tell me "heads up" to a possible situation with that group. Neither Mrs. Pierce nor I wanted to tackle those potential troublemakers. We knew it would be asking for more problems than we could handle. So, following her lead I looked for help. Help was close by in the form of security guards. Keeping with our method of non-verbal communication, I motioned with my hand to get their attention. This was followed by slightly moving my head, thus notifying the guards to look in the direction of the boys.

By now other students were watching the group with increasing interest. Having witnessed rumbles in the past, they could guess what was about to happen. Now I was caught up in the predicament of whether to call 911 immediately or wait. I decided waiting would waste precious time. Thinking about what could happen if this situation got out of hand, I signaled to a teacher close to the door, alerting her to a possible emergency in our presence. My method of conveying a crisis to her was to form my thumb and pinky into the shape of a phone. Silently, I mouthed the words "Call 911."

Our call for help took place not a minute too soon. Loud voices erupted from the huddle of boys. Each youngster was yelling curses and trying to project his voice over the others. Drugs seemed to be at the center of the dispute. Unfortunately, it usually is when there is a big altercation among older kids. Of course there are those times, though few in number, where you will have a ruckus with boys over a girl that they both liked or over some other type of nonsense. But the major disputes in the neighborhood that turned seriously ugly would be over drugs and/or owed money. Instinctively, I began to herd the students away from the trouble. Most of them had already started to move towards the door in anticipation of a fight. But there were those few who had no fear and nosiness outweighed common sense. None of us knew if weapons were involved. And no one wanted to have to deal with stray bullets that could be fired indiscriminately.

Sirens could be heard in the distance. That was great to hear; we needed help, and fast. By now all four of those fools were swinging and connecting with some very heavy punches. "Hurry . . . hurry!" I found myself actually hollering those words down the block through the chain linked fence at the approaching police cars. They couldn't hear me but yelling made me feel better. By now most of the student body had sought refuge inside the building. Our security guards were doing their best but they were no match for those warriors. Their method of passive resistance just wasn't working. They were trying to stop the fight by talking, holding, and separating them, not by aggressive techniques such as punching and kicking. Weird as it might seem, it appeared that our fighters switched sides in the middle of their battle and joined forces to fight against our security guards. Fighting fire with fire is not always a good action to implement. But in this case our guards needed to kick butts in order to become victorious. By the time they changed their approach to the dispute and decided to return aggression, it was too late. Security ended up getting the most severe injuries out of the group.

When it was all over, two of our security guards were taken to the hospital. One had a broken hand, the other a fractured jaw. The boys that started the fight refused medical attention even though they probably needed it. The four fighters were taken to police headquarters where they were interrogated, which was done with their parents' permission. No one would reveal what the disagreement was about. They were eventually charged with assault and released into the custody of their parents. Since all four had police records, we heard this offense might carry a heavier sentence. Also, since two adults were involved and injured, this meant an additional charge was added on. Nevertheless, something positive came out of this terrible situation; the fighters that attended our school were expelled and could not return to Bradley. We were elated to hear that we wouldn't have to put up with their disorderly conduct anymore. It might have been a selfish attitude but we figured they now became some other educator's problem. Life in our school would be just a little easier for the teachers, deans, and especially the security guards.

CHAPTER 36

Easter was late this year. As a result, we were looking forward to our vacation during the 3rd week of April. We were only nine days away and I could hardly wait. The students couldn't contain their excitement either. They were eagerly anticipating time away from their teachers, the watchful staff and, surprisingly, from one another. But, just like the Christmas and Thanksgiving holidays where students were on their best behavior, we were hoping for the same docile atmosphere as we entered the Easter season. So, once again, we noticed an effort by the students to minimize all arguments, fights and any other disputes that would cause the deans to send for their parents. Regrettably, nothing is perfect. Two students did not feel compelled to pay attention to the *"let's be good"* policy that the rest of the student body wisely adhered to. During today's lunch period, one of the nastiest confrontations of my career took place which could have cost a student his life.

The seventh graders were in the cafeteria. When I entered the lunch room I was acutely aware of the calm and quiet that surrounded me. This was so unlike the unrelenting roar of voices that always greeted my ears. Most days I listened to yelling across the room, uncontrollably high-pitched laughter and loud conversations. Today, students were silently eating with only an occasional chuckle or low whisper. What in the world was going on??? Mr. Brathwaite, the teacher on lunch duty, nodded in my direction as he entered the room. I acknowledged his hello with my own nod in return. The doors noisily flung open and Mr. Kay's class entered. They were labeled the terrors of the school. Mr. Kay always got the worse classes. That's the way he liked it. He didn't want the smart and well-disciplined children. He always said that teaching them was dull and no challenge to a teacher's creative abilities. Kay only taught this one class for the entire day; and he always escorted his class everywhere they went because they couldn't be trusted. Even to the cafeteria he was their constant guide. They always entered wearing their egos on their shoulders; making their presence known with their boisterous promenade around the room to the back tables. So, today was no exception. In fact, today they sounded rowdier than ever. This was more noticeable because of the quiet room. The students as well as the faculty thought that some kids in Kay's class were a little weird. In fact, statements like "Ron's not operating with a full deck or James is one French fry short of a happy meal" were heard from time to time. Honestly, I had to agree with those comments. I could recall a few strange students that I had to handle while teaching his classes, too. I must admit, though, Kay had a way with handling those difficult kids. One day he told me that his secret was to start each school term, from the very first day, with certain "rituals." "Rituals" was the term he used to describe, in a single word, the tactics used to keep order in his classroom. He believed in fighting fire with fire and felt that the teachers that did not employ this method of control lost the battle before it began. I completely agreed with his approach to discipline and even copied some of his techniques when needed. For one, I keep laughing with students at a minimum; and as I've expressed before, when a student is known to have a weapon on his person, using words like "please" can get you hurt or even killed. You must relate to the particular problem in a strong, positive manner. It was known that Mr. Kay would tell students that were threats to others, or a student he assumed might have a weapon,

"Sit your ass down before I stomp it down", or "unless you want the shit knocked out of you, I strongly advise you to chill out."

One time when he was up against a student trying to stab his classmate, I heard him say, "You don't want me to lose my size 15's on you where the sun don't shine, do you? If not, you'd better back your ass off!"

It worked! The student retreated to a neutral area of the room dropping the knife on the floor as he walked. Of course, most of the time he was in a defensive situation when he yelled those words; or . . . he was dealing with life threatening circumstances. The best part was the students knew he meant what he said. They also knew he could deliver what he promised. Standing 6'4" and weighing a whopping 314 pounds, he was definitely an impressive figure to behold. It was no wonder Kay rarely had to use physical force to stop an altercation. His booming voice and huge size were his weapons. We all appreciated his presence when something serious was happening. Anyway, my motto was, "whatever works," and his so-called "rituals" were well respected by his class. Of course, that didn't mean they respected other teachers. Kay headed in my direction.

"How's it going, Lawson?"

It was common practice for most teachers to address each other without the title Mr., Mrs. or Ms. I responded to Kay's greeting with,

"Very peaceful until your guys came in."

His chuckle told me he found my statement amusing. "They do liven up a place, don't they!"

He turned and looked at his class. They seemed to be split into two sides and participating in a group argument. "Hey, simmer down,"

Kay boomed this command in a thunderous voice. His tone got an immediate reaction. Everyone looked at him and then lowered their voices.

"My goodness . . . they certainly pay you a lot of
R-E-S-P-E-C-T,"

I spelled out the word as I softly sang the melody to Aretha Franklin's song. Again, he chuckled, this time with a little more volume. He responded as I was just getting warmed up into the second verse,

"find out what it means to me."

"They're smart! They know not to get on my bad side."

With those words he turned to leave saying that he would be back to pick them up before the end of the period.

CHAPTER 37

It didn't take long before the lunchroom staff and I realized we were in trouble. One by one Kay's students began to notice that their teacher was no longer present. Within seconds the voice levels rose and the class dispute continued where they had left off.

"What in the world are they in such an uproar about?" I remarked to Mrs. Brunson, another teacher on lunch duty.

I learned from her about a conversation she overheard concerning two students, Jean and Tyrone, who appeared to be at the center of the dispute. By straining my ears in their direction, I could also pick up bits and pieces of the argument. That's how I managed to overhear Tyrone utter . . .

"This bitch had no right messing in my business."

Oh oh! In any language those were fighting words. He might not have been yelling, but the word "bitch" came through loud and clear. Immediately Jean jumped to her feet knocking over her chair.

"Maybe I didn't hear him right, so, somebody *pleeese* correct me if I'm making a mistake! Did that mother fucker call me a *bitch?*"

Unlike Tyrone's remark, Jean's words were very loud. In fact, everyone in the room heard her nerve-racking shriek. A gut feeling sent me quickly moving in Jean's direction. I've been a dean long enough to smell a fight in the making. Believe me, my nose has come in handily in other situations like this. Braithwaite must have a refined nose detector, too, because out of the corner of my eye I could see him joining me in a race to prevent a lunchroom riot. Social skills are down the toilet during times like these. Even the good students get involved with lunchroom drama and agitators use this time as prime opportunity to do their own mischief. We reached Jean a second too late to stop her retaliation to Tyrone's unkind words. Picking up the chair that she knocked over, Jean swung it over her head and viciously struck Tyrone with tremendous force, knocking him and his chair to the floor. She was still screaming vulgarities as she attacked him. Braithwaite and I reached the table at the same time. I grabbed Jean and he snatched the chair from her grasp before she could land the second blow. Looking down I was happy to see that Tyrone was moving and trying to get up. At least she hadn't killed him. Jean displayed no remorse. When she realized he was alert and could hear her, she nastily snarled,

"How do you like what this *bitch* did to your ass now, mother fucker?"

A loud cheer was heard from all the girls in her class in approval. I'm sure I don't have to tell you that the boys viewed the attack on their friend quite differently.

"Hey, watssup with that, bitch?" one boy yelled trying to get past the security guards that had arrived.

Security had entered in front of the school nurse a few seconds after Jean's attack on Tyrone. A friend standing close to Tyrone took a better look at his head while the nurse was applying ice to the huge lump that was steadily rising on his temple. He made a report to the rest of the group.

"Don't sweat it, y'all. He gonna be awwite."

I turned and took a good look at the student that spoke. It never ceased to amaze me how these students invented their own language no matter how hard we, as educators, tried to correct and change their way of speaking. English teachers, like me, have a harder time coping with the generation speech gap.

By now security had taken Jean away and the paramedics were preparing to transport Tyrone to the hospital. Taking a deep breath I glanced around the room. Surprisingly none of the other students in the cafeteria had moved. They observed the action from their seats and cooperated when asked to remain seated until Tyrone was removed to the ambulance. I released the students before the late bell rang with instructions to hurry, but not run, to their next period class. An announcement was made over the intercom to allow the seventh graders an extra three-minute traveling time to their classes. Kay's class remained with me until he came for them. By then they had calmed down. They silently followed him out of the cafeteria fully aware that they would receive the lecture of their life when they reached their classroom.

Tyrone was examined in the hospital's emergency room and admitted overnight for observation. Luckily, he was not seriously injured. Except for the egg size bump on his head, he was in good shape. His parents were nice enough not to press charges, therefore Jean was not arrested. Instead, she was suspended for five days and had to go to counseling along with anger management classes.

I was told that Jean's mother punished her for two months. Her mother told her that sixty days punishment was nothing compared to what she could have received if she had killed Tyrone. Mom's statement was on the money! When will society learn that, "sticks and stones can break their bones but **words** can never harm them." If Jean had governed her actions by that rule, she definitely would have had a more enjoyable Easter vacation.

CHAPTER 38

"Hindsight is 20-20." Now, that's a proverb that brings back memories from my younger years. I can still hear my mother's lecture on the virtues of being able to avoid the pitfalls in life that hang around waiting to engulf us. Another one of mom's favorite sayings was "think before you leap." The quote is supposed to actually say "look before you leap." However, my mother always gave adages her own special flavor.

"Betty, you are too impetuous," were the words she always used to begin my scolding after I made a rash decision. "You must consider the consequences of your actions before you make a move."

I vividly remember one incident in particular when I was in a game of follow the leader on skates.

I was a fearless ten-year-old who felt nothing bad could happen to me. Did I find out the hard way how wrong I was. As I waited my turn to speed skate down the block, ending climatically by jumping over a log, I briefly thought of the damage I could do to my body if I failed to successfully clear that piece of wood. My turn was up and the success of the other five skaters gave me sufficient motivation to try my luck. Besides, I didn't want to be laughed at by my friends or be called a scared baby. You guessed it . . . my right toe hit the log causing my face to be painfully introduced to the pavement. Talk about hurt, embarrassment and anger! I felt it all. I scraped my chin, cut my knee and badly busted my lip. To add to all my misery, I had to go home and listen to a long, long lecture from my mother about the lack of thought I gave to my own safety when I decided to play that game.

What my mother didn't know was I did think about getting hurt. But due to peer pressure, the threat of pain was not sufficient to stop me from participating. As mom tended to my bruises, her speech continued for approximately 30 minutes and ended with, "The day will come when I'm not going to be around to remind you about what you need to do to safeguard yourself. You've got to use what's in that object on top of your shoulders. It's not up there just to be used as a decoration, you know."

Her words didn't make my suffering any easier. And I was in too much pain to give much credence to the meaning. But as I now reflected on the decisions I made on a balmy April afternoon, my mother's words came back to haunt me.

CHAPTER 39

It was the end of a strenuous week full of discipline problems. To make matters worse, it was Friday the 13th complete with a full moon eerily hovering above. This spooky day crept up on us right after we returned from our Easter vacation. Everyone was expecting a double dose of misery from the students. However, we were pleasantly surprised by a rather cooperative student body. Except for a few minor disputes, the day rolled by rather smoothly.

"The day's not over yet" I jokingly shouted to a group of teachers who passed me in the hall.

"Don't jinx us," Ms. Patterson yelled back.

At the end of the hall, they separated and I continued my patrol.

Twenty minutes later the first bell rang sending students hustling to their homerooms to prepare for dismissal. A few minutes later the last bell sounded allowing students to leave the building.

Most teachers never leave at three o'clock. Some put the next day's lessons on the board. Others make sure their classrooms are in order after the onset of 150 youngsters. Deans also have the "3 o'clock blues." The suspension business was good. We received students quicker than we could deplete our paper piles. This meant our desks were always loaded with uncompleted paperwork concerning disruptive students. Before returning to my room, I always patrolled the halls on my floor, making sure there were no stragglers hiding in the building. On this particular day, everything was quiet on the fourth floor. Trying to maintain the exhilarated feeling I had all afternoon, I decided to ignore my stack of papers and leave school early. Unfortunately, I didn't have a clue to what awaited me as I headed for my car or I would have gladly spent the night in the building. Looking back, I realized I should have followed the advice of my colleague and kept walking until I had safely reached my car.

The piercing screams that penetrated the block froze me in one spot. Glancing over my left shoulder I saw a woman in a panic, running down the block with a baby in her arms screaming for help. She was dressed only in her panties and bra. Her feet were bare and her baby was wearing only a diaper. Behind her was a fully dressed man wielding a belt like a circus animal trainer, occasionally cracking it like a whip. Each time the belt connected with her body her screams would go from loud to piercing. I was mortified at what I saw; and thought that they were crazy to be out here practically naked in this weather. It was April 29th and one of the coldest days in the month. In fact, a few weeks ago we had snow flurries. It didn't last long; however, winter was obviously not over yet.

My Goodness . . . did you see that? He almost hit the baby in the face," I shouted to the person walking past my still motionless body.

"Mind your business, Lawson. The police won't even get into domestic situations. Knowing you, you'll probably stick your nose into this mess and end up getting it chopped off."

I saw that it was Paula Dooley, supervisor of the computer department, offering the advice. She spoke as she quickly walked by, never breaking her stride.

"I know you, Missy." By this time she had passed me and had to raise her voice to be heard. Slightly turning but still walking, she continued . . .

"You get involved in problems that are sometimes unsolvable. Something tells me this is one of those issues that you can't win. You'll be flirting with disaster trying to help these people. Believe me when I tell you that they don't want to be helped. Been there . . . done that . . . and I'm tired of wearing that damn tee shirt over and over again. Go home, Lawson . . . *go home!*"

The second, "go home," was so loud she practically screamed it at me. Ignoring her warning I turned and headed across the street toward the row of three-story buildings that lined the opposite side of the block. How could Paula be so callous? Being a woman herself, you would expect her to be more sympathetic. Increasing my speed, I began pacing my steps so that I would reach the opposite side at the same time as the approaching woman. She was still running, sometimes into the street in order to dodge the sting of the belt. By now she was moving with a limp. Viewing me as a barrier from the vicious beating she was receiving, she disappeared behind me allowing me to come face to face with her abuser.

Lucky for me, three male teachers started across the street to assist me in the standoff. Outnumbered, the man stopped about ten feet in front of me. It was clear that he was checking his options and concluded that to continue pursuing this course of action was not in his best interest. Muttering a few curse words which were accompanied by a very nasty glance in my direction, he turned and hurried into his building. An uncomfortable feeling spread throughout my body. His exit performance displayed that he was sending a message that was meant to scare me. His eyes also conveyed that I would have been at the receiving end of that belt if my colleagues had not come to assist me. That definitely was not a comforting thought. *Now*, what do I do? I couldn't just leave as if nothing happened. Where would this poor woman go? Not back inside that house where he could kill her and maybe even harm the baby. I decided to call an agency for battered women who suffer from domestic violence. So holding the crying woman by the arm, I headed back to the school.

CHAPTER 40

Dialing the domestic violence agency became a chore. "Calls from clients must be outrageous, "I remarked with an irritation in my voice. I was speaking to Janell, who had just stuck her head into the first-floor office that I had commandeered.

"What's going on?" Her voice started loud but trailed off into an inaudible whisper.

She glanced around the room observing the sobbing woman holding a very bewildered looking infant. They were draped in a blanket I found in the nurses' room. At least she wasn't shivering anymore. Finding out that my troubled guest only spoke Spanish was not helping the circumstances. My Spanish was a little rusty but I still was able to find out her name and that she had five children. She also told me that her husband would beat her anytime he felt like it. She said he was especially vicious after he had a few beers. By his actions, I would guess that today must have been a big beer day. I translated this information for Janell. I then said to her, "I'm having a hard time reaching the agency that helps battered women. I've tried dialing six times without any success." Janell thought for a minute then said, "I might have a different number that could work. Guidance Counselors are given direct numbers to many of the agencies."

Janell reached into her bag, pulled out her organizer, and quickly flipped through the pages.

"Ah hah . . . found it!" She rattled off the number while I dialed. It was music to my ears to hear the phone ring instead of that annoying busy signal. A friendly operator directed my call to a counselor. I informed him of the problem and was told that he would send someone to pick the woman up within an hour. After asking me if I would be able to handle this by myself, Janell left as quickly as she entered. She said something about being late for an appointment. After her departure, I called my house to tell my husband why I would be late and to take the kids out for a fast-food dinner.

Almost three hours later a representative walked through the door. By now, I was beside myself with frustration and anger. The baby had no food or clean diapers, and I had no clothes or food for either of them. I was afraid to leave them alone to get what they needed for fear of the angry man across the street. So, by the time the representative arrived I had a difficult time restraining myself from saying,

"Traffic from Jupiter must have been a bitch." But I managed to keep my mouth shut. The clock read 6:42

p.m. By now everyone had gone home except for me and the custodial staff. To add to my discomfort, I was informed by the representative that I would probably receive a subpoena to appear in court to testify in the case. I was not a happy camper upon hearing this news. I definitely was upset with myself and felt that Paula Dooley was right when she told me I should mind my own business. On the other hand, I keep reminding myself that I might have saved two lives by intervening.

I was happy to see that they sent a representative that spoke fluent Spanish. At the completion of her interview, the mother and child were escorted to a car and driven to a shelter. The representative's departing words to me were, "You'll be hearing from me soon. We're going to really need your input with this case."

We all left together at 7:24 p.m. When we exited the building we could see the husband watching us through the blinds. I had to walk a block to my car. I could feel the abuser's eyes following me which was not a good feeling. All he did was watch. I was hoping this was a sign that he was learning to control his temper. I silently celebrated and gave myself an imaginary "high five" when I reached my car unharmed and drove off the block.

CHAPTER 41

The next few weeks I felt like I was trapped in a whirlwind and there was no escape. As predicted, I was deeply involved with Mrs. Jamez, the lady I rescued from her abusive husband. Taking care of my responsibilities as dean and making two appearances in court within three weeks was a lot for me to handle. But handle it I did. Both of those court appearances were a waste of time. Neither Mrs. Jamez nor her husband showed and I wasted a lot of time sitting on a court bench waiting for them to keep their appointments. Then, I had to deal with the "I told you so" remarks from my colleagues. Paula Dooley was especially vocal since she was the person who tried to get me to go home on that ill-fated day in April.

"Lawson," she said authoritatively upon entering my office one morning, "You mean well. Because of your personality, you make a fantastic dean. Even though you're tough, the kids still like and respect you. Now, that's saying a lot when you have these kids on your side. I realize you felt that I was heartless when I tried to get you to go home. What you don't know is that I was speaking from experience. Without going into detail, I was in a situation similar to yours a few years ago. It almost cost me my job. I don't want to see that happen to you. I can see myself in you.

If you're not careful, you will get slaughtered by these people along with getting caught up in their confused lives. Anyway, it's too late to turn back now. You have committed yourself, and now you have to see it through to the end. Good luck, Lawson. Honestly, I mean it. I really wish you well with this case. But, of course, you realize that the worst is yet to come. You might need all the luck you can get before it's all over. So, if there's anything I can do to help you, just let me know." With those words she waved goodbye and left my office.

After she was gone, I thought about what she said and the questions she left unanswered. What did she mean by "the worst is yet to come?" Did she know something that I didn't know? Shouldn't I find out what it is before it's too late? I appreciated her offer of support, but I knew that I was on my own to finish this problem. I had an appointment with the court in eight days. The district attorney said this would be the last time I would have to appear. So, I kept my fingers crossed that everything turned out well. I still saw the Jamezes on the block each work day. Apparently, she reunited with her husband. I am always puzzled by the decisions of women like Mrs. Jamez. He practically put her in the hospital, yet she goes back home with forgiveness in her heart.

Eight days later I found myself waiting on a bench outside the courtroom one more time. I saw the Jamezes arrive together, and they were escorted into a side room. It looked like this time we were going to have a trial. All of a sudden, my stomach became tense and felt like it was full of butterflies. By the time I was called to testify, I was a nervous wreck. The attorneys were kind to me. Neither the district attorney nor the defense lawyer was ruthless during the interrogation process. I was out of the court room and back on the hall bench within twenty minutes. Leaning my head back with my eyes closed, I was just beginning to unwind when the door opened and everyone filed out of the courtroom.

Looking up, I spotted Mr. and Mrs. Jamez in the middle of the crowd. They walked pass me, both staring at me with hatred in their eyes. Suddenly Mrs. Jamez stopped and turned around. In almost perfect English she yelled at me, "You bitch . . . why the hell didn't you mind your own damn business. I hate you." She then followed her laughing husband out of the building. I did not move. I couldn't because I was too shocked at what had just happened.

Deeply hurt and astounded at what just occurred, I don't know what surprised me the most. The fact that she cursed me out after I tried to help her; or her ability to speak perfect English with practically no accent. I believe the latter won. Could it be that Paula anticipated this sort of feedback from the Jamez family? That would explain her warning. Being elusive about her past incidents with volatile groups was probably her way of trying not to prejudice my opinion on the case.

"Don't take what she said personally."

Looking around at the person taking the empty seat next to me, I recognized the representative from the battered women's organization. I hadn't seen her since the evening she came to my school to rescue Mrs. Jamez. She must have noticed the shocked look that was still on my face.

"She's upset because her children were temporarily placed in a foster home for their own protection. As expected, her welfare money was cut off when her children were removed. She blames you for everything that happened, instead of her husband who is the real culprit. Her outburst is totally about the money; that's all. By the way, I believe you will find it interesting to know that she returned to her husband the very next day after we picked her up. You know, we can't force her to stay away from her abuser. But we can save her children from being subjected to her type of life style. That's where you came in. The reason the DA sent you a subpoena was because we needed your help to protect her children. Your testimony was paramount in making a case against the Jamezes. I'm just sorry you had to be caught in the middle of this mess."

Taking my leave, I thanked her for the information and left the building.

That day I wearily left the courthouse. I was not looking forward to facing my colleagues. As you would expect, I am going to have to endure more "I told you so" from everybody. Even my husband felt I was foolish to become so entangled in those people's lives.

Now that the trial had ended and my school life was back to normal, I had time to think about all that happened in the past weeks. I also recalled the lectures my mom used to give me. If she were alive, I could imagine how she would react to my involvement in this case.

"Betty," she'd say, "you're doing it again! Did you investigate the facts all the way through before you jumped in with both feet? You know, you should have figured that she would go back to her husband. Anyway, experience is the best teacher. Now that you've made your mistake, just make sure you don't fall into the same trap again." It was almost like she was here talking to me.

The Jamez family moved two weeks later. I couldn't have been happier. I was tired of feeling like there was a bull's-eye on my back while entering and exiting the block. Since my recent involvement with the Jamez family, I have had many discussions with myself. One of my favorite topics to scrutinize is that same case. I always ask myself . . . If another crisis arose like the one across the street, and being more knowledgeable now than you were before about life, would you get involved? My answer was always the same. I probably would!

CHAPTER 42

The month of May has always been a difficult time for us. The smell of spring was in the air and the students were excitedly responding to the beautiful weather. Flowers were blooming and puppy love was flourishing all over the school. We definitely had to keep an eye on excessive student activity which could be anywhere. We kept a surveillance on the halls, stairwells, empty classrooms and any other nooks and crannies that offered solitude for hanky panky. This time of year hormones were raging out of control. The outcome of these uncontrollable emotions is cocky young men and eager to please young women. That spelled trouble. That also meant we had to be cognizant of the triangle affairs that could bloom from all of these mixed-up relationships. Troubles always arose when one boy was "talking" to two girls. That combination always produced disastrous results . . . especially if sex was involved.

"What a gorgeous day," I reflected as I left home that sunny morning in the middle of the month. The flowers in my yard seemed to be smiling at me as I passed the front gate walking to my car. My mood was a festive one due to the fact that I was driving a new car. Yes, I finally replaced my ride since my other car was demolished in December by the kid escaping from the police. The drive to work was pleasant. The day continued with the same pleasing atmosphere. First, second and third periods slipped by like a breeze. No incidents, no problems, all students in their classes.

Lunchtime brought happy noises from students still reveling in the aroma of a delightful spring morning, and eager to spend their cafeteria time engaged in stimulating conversation about who was dating whom. My floor was finally empty and quiet from the hustle and bustle of students' movement. At least, that's what I thought. Leaning back in my chair, I sat in my office enjoying the silence.

"Bitches, I'll slice you up like pieces of meat."

"Damn, where did that come from," I swiftly jumped out of my chair and rushed to the door.

Looking to my left I saw a woman with two young girls, probably her daughters, all three looking pass me toward the end of the hall. To my right I recognized a youngster named Candy, one of our problem students. I've always wondered why they named that child Candy. I like candy and there was certainly nothing likable or sweet about this child. She was the leader of a neighborhood female gang. She had a big mouth and a bad attitude. Plus, she was no bigger than a minute. That was the name the old folks gave to very small people. Looking at this tiny young female, I always wondered why a group of girls thought she was tough enough to be their leader. Obviously, any of her followers would win in a hand-to-hand combat.

"Did you hear what I said, Bitch? Don't think I'm 'fraid of y'all just cause you got your old lady with you. I ain't scared of her either."

Neither the mother nor her two daughters responded to Candy's nasty words. I stepped away from the privacy of my doorway and into the hall. I was hoping my presence would defuse the situation before it became a bigger problem. What I did know was that Mom and daughters were lucky that I decided to rest in my office a little longer. Most days I would have been on duty in the lunchroom by now. Taking note that my room was halfway between the group on the left and Candy on my right I stood there glaring at the small youngster with the vulgar mouth. I could tell that she was surprised to see me. However, my presence made no difference in how she controlled her actions. Instead of retreating, Candy began to slowly walk in my direction still yelling curses and insults. I knew her ultimate aim was to reach the people standing at the other end of the hall. But to reach them she had to get past me. I wondered how she planned to accomplish that feat. I didn't have long to wait for my answer.

When she was within arm's length from me, she suddenly made a dash missing my grasp by inches. She moved like lightning with me hot on her heels. I knew I had to catch her. I also knew nothing good would happen if she reached those people. Candy was half my size which made her twice as fast. But I was hoping that I could still count on some skills left from my high school days on the track team. Even though that was many years ago, on occasion my speed had aided me in catching other students. Today was my lucky day!

She tripped over her own feet which resulted in her stumbling and temporarily slowing down. That pause was all I needed to give me the edge required to catch her. Using my body I slammed her into the wall. She had speed but her small frame was no match for my size 38 hips. She careened into the wall, bounced off like a ball and ended up in a sitting position on the ground. Something fell out of her jacket sleeve as she was sinking to the floor. She picked it up, but I quickly reached down and yanked the switch blade from her grasp just as she was about to open it. She

Looked up at me with fire in her eyes. Evidently, I spoiled her plans to have a rumble on the fourth floor. Subsequently, her next move was a big shocker which left me speechless. Candy proceeded to call me every filthy name in the book. I must admit, some of those names I never even heard of before. What a repulsive kid! I had to smother the urge to smack her in her foul mouth. I looked around at the other team, making sure they had not moved from their positions. I didn't want them taking advantage of this interlude as a chance to repay Candy by using some of her own methods. There was no need for me to worry. Three statues were staring at Candy. In fact, they appeared to be petrified to that one spot. Plus, fear was written across all three faces. We all silently watched Candy slowly rise to her feet. It was frightening for me to observe how this enraged youngster never took her eyes off the three figures at the end of the hall. But luckily for her she didn't try to attack them anymore; all she did was stare.

CHAPTER 43

Leaving mom and her daughters in my office, I sent Candy packing with a five-day suspension. Security then transported her to the main office to be picked up by her mom. I wanted the principal to handle this one. After being cursed out by her, I didn't want to have to deal with her anymore. My reaction toward this student couldn't be trusted at this time, especially if she gave me a repeat performance from her mouth. Besides, I wanted her out of the school for the rest of that day and maybe for the rest of the school year. I definitely was going to lobby for her to be transferred to another school. Meanwhile, I had to deal with the trauma that Candy caused to her three victims.

After everything had quieted down, I spoke to the two young ladies and their mom. They said that they never realized how dangerous their ex-friend was. That's right! They all used to be best friends and in the same gang. This was verified by the mom and her daughters. My lunch hour was spent talking to Mrs. Crawford, Janeese and Jametta. Problems with Candy started when she and Jametta were involved with the same boy. Apparently, Candy found out and told him he had to choose one of them. He chose Jametta. Candy became enraged and wanted to fight her, but Jametta and her sister got away and ran home. Personally, I feel Candy didn't stand a chance against the sisters. One could have beaten her in a fight never mind both of them together. After Mrs. Crawford found out about the gang, she demanded that her daughters not be involved with Candy and her friends. Having your boyfriend reject you for your friend and then that same friend's mom rejects you, make for a big problem. Candy felt "disrespected" and told everyone she was going to get even with the two bitches and their mother.

Mrs. Crawford heard about the threat and came to school for help. She feared for her daughters' welfare and wanted the school to intercede on their behalf. But before the mother could speak to anyone, the altercation took place in the hall. She said she didn't know what else to do, and if today was any indication of things to come, she knew that they were still in trouble. Naturally, I sent for Janell. Both Janell and I convinced Mrs. Crawford to go to the police station and file a complaint against Candy. The school supported her by putting in our own incident report. Mrs. Crawford and her children left with Janell to continue their strategy discussion before visiting the precinct. We all came to the same conclusion. That gang of bullies had to be disbanded before someone was seriously injured. If the school and the community allowed those girls to continue their reign of terror, then we would be partly responsible for whatever misery they might bring forth to the neighborhood.

The following week, Janell approached me in the teachers' cafeteria with good news. With the help of the police department, Candy's gang had been disbanded. Apparently, news of the school incident had reached the parents of her gang members. Then shortly afterward, the gang and their parents were visited by our local police. Those parents immediately confronted their own children, getting the whole story behind Candy's attempted assault. They also questioned their daughters on what part they might have played in the school episode. After they were satisfied that they had gotten all the information out of their children, the mothers gathered at one house for a united meeting with all the girls. At this time, they made a combined decision not to allow their daughters to associate with Candy. They even went as far as apologizing to Mrs. Crawford for their children's behavior and had their daughters write letters to ask forgiveness for their terrible actions.

Candy had finally lost her power. After her suspension was completed, she came back to school a changed child. When she entered my office accompanied by her mother, I couldn't believe that this was the same human being that cursed me out. Candy walked in with her head down and did not sit until I offered her a seat. She apologized for her behavior and promised that it would not happen again. Mrs. Sands told me that she had heard that I was putting pressure on the administration to get her daughter out of our school. She begged me to give Candy another chance and guaranteed that I would have no more trouble out of her child. I watched Candy closely throughout the entire meeting in my office. She seemed to be truly sorry for what she said to me and appeared to be remorseful for her past actions against her friends. Consequently, after a long pause, I said that I would cancel my complaint to have her daughter discharged from Bradley Middle School. However, both Candy and Mrs. Sands were put on notice; anymore problems from Candy, there would be no more discussion. She would have to go. I would personally lead the committee that requested her expulsion. They both nodded and stated that they understood the terms and Candy agreed to abide by the conditions.

I watched her walk out of my office. With the slouching of her head and shoulders, Candy's body language told me all I needed to know. Candy looked like she didn't have a friend in the world . . . and she probably didn't. Analyzing Mrs. Sands' posture told me that she was thoroughly humiliated by her daughter's actions and would have liked to bury her head like an ostrich if it were at all possible. I could only hope for Mrs. Sands' sake, that Candy was on the path to rehabilitation and was able to keep the promise she made to me today. I definitely would be keeping an eye on her progress.

CHAPTER 44

We were in the last weeks of the school term. June was finally here and everyone in the school was in high spirits. I was sitting in my office once again trying to catch up with the huge mound of paperwork. Piercing voices interrupted my thoughts from the quiet hallway.

"Who's bringing the potato salad?" a husky voice said, a little too loudly.

"Don't know, but I signed up to bring paper plates," another voice said, in response.

"I hope Joan's making the potato salad. She makes some g-o-o-o-d salad."

"When did you taste her salad? Was it at last year's party?"

"Yep . . . sure did!" she confirmed.

This conversation was taking place outside my office. Peeking out of my door window, I saw two colleagues meandering down the hall. I gathered they were discussing the school's end of the year party and who was bringing what. They were in no hurry and seemed to be pacing their steps to coincide with the first bell. In the past years, we all went to a chic restaurant and had a great time enjoying the fancy cuisine and each other's company. Last year we did the catering ourselves and it was proven that there were good chefs among the staff. So because of our fantastic cooks, I can tell that it is going to be hard to get these people to try restaurant get-togethers again.

They unanimously voted to have the staff cater our party for a second year. This was the first week in June and vacation time was rapidly approaching. Just two more weeks until the last day of the term. Since the two ladies discussing the menu were co-chairs of the food committee and the teachers at the school's cooking classes, it sounded to me as if they weren't going to rest until they had everything perfect. Even if that meant bugging people until they got what they wanted. I needed to walk the halls, but I didn't dare leave my office until they had left my floor.

Without being seen, I peeked through the glass window one more time. Don't get me wrong, I was planning to contribute to the party, but I didn't want to get into a full scaled description of what I was planning to bring right now. I wasn't sure whether I wanted to cook something or purchase my donation, ready-made, from the store. I definitely didn't want any advice on what they thought I should bring. So, I continued to secretly watch them as they slowly strolled to the end of the hall. There they stopped and for two or three more minutes continued their chatter on what delicious dishes they would like to see at the affair.

"Brrring . . . brrring . . . . brrring . . . . Brrring . . . brrring . . . . brrring."

"Oh no, not again! That's the emergency bell. This is the first time in months that Mr. Ballentine had to sound that alarm."

I noticed I was speaking aloud to myself again. That bell didn't ring often, but when it did it usually meant big problems for somebody. Mr. Ballentine's voice came over the intercom with instructions.

"We are expecting a visitor on the fourth floor. Please make sure you contact the main office concerning the procedures that must be taken if the visitor appears without a pass. All assistant principals and deans need to contact me for further clarification."

That was a confusing message. What visitor? And why were there emergency bells concerning this visitor? The fourth floor was my floor. I needed a little more information on our mysterious visitor and how we were supposed to handle him or her. It would help if we knew whether our visitor was male or female. Calling the main office proved to be an impossible task. It seems as if I wasn't the only person trying to get through to the principal to get an explanation on this unknown guest. After three tries, I gave up and decided to call Action Jackson. He picked up immediately and by his tone I could tell he was amused about something. "Heello," he practically sang the word. I wondered what made him sound so happy.

"Action, this is Betty. Do you have any more information about the message Mr. Ballentine just relayed to us?" I could hear him laughing as he answered me.

"I most certainly do," he chuckled obviously trying to maintain his composure. All of a sudden, he gave up his struggle and broke into a hearty laughter.

"What in the devil is so funny?" I asked. "How about letting me in on the joke? You know, I like a good laugh, too."

Now, he really became over zealously loud. What in the world did I just say to cause this reaction? I decided to wait patiently until he got whatever was bugging him out of his system. Leaning back in my chair I remained quiet until his enthusiastic snickering had subsided. He finally spoke, words tumbling out in-between hiccups and sporadic short breaths.

"You know (pause) I'm just imagining (pause) what your face is going to look like (pause) when I tell you (pause) who our guest is. I'd give fifty bucks, no . . . let me change that to one hundred dollars to be sitting across from you this very moment instead of on the phone. But, since I won't be able to see your expression or reaction, I'm using my imagination . . . which is almost as good. Okay, I think I have control of myself. Well . . . here goes! The snake in the science lab has escaped. They're not sure where he is. You know, snakes are quite versatile. They're able to mold their bodies into all types of shapes so that they can fit into smaller spaces and objects. I have always found that fact interesting. Hello . . . hello . . . Betty, you still there?"

I don't think I heard anything Action said after the words *snake and escape*. I **hated** those creepy crawling things. Bugs, caterpillars, centipedes, spiders and mice . . . for me they all fall into the category of nauseating things. But *snakes* are at the top of the "nauseating things" list. I'm sure most people in the world would agree with me. Laughter brought me back to reality and the fact that I was still on the phone. There he goes again! Because he wasn't afraid, he found this whole episode amusing. I surely didn't! I began to question him faster than he could answer.

"Did I hear you right? You did say a snake has escaped, didn't you? Where did they last see it? In what direction was it headed? Whose fault was this, anyway?"

By now Action was laughing so hard he brought on a coughing spell. Damn him, damn that snake, damn everybody responsible for that snake's escape. Whose bright idea was it to authorize having snakes in a school? This was no place for those ugly things. This could be worse than the invasion of the pit bulls! Without saying goodbye, I hung up on Action in the middle of his jovial breakdown. I didn't need to hear anymore from him. Now, what should I do? Should I go home until it was caught? No, that won't work. I heard somewhere that snakes could live in the walls and come out when they wanted to get air or needed to look for food. It could be lost in this building forever. Maybe I should ask for a leave of absence or just quit my job. Okay, now I'm being ridiculous. I had too much invested in Bradley to let a snake chase me out of the building. Besides, I would miss the relationships I had developed over the years. That included Action Jackson even though at this very moment I was furious with him for thinking this whole catastrophe was funny. It looks like I was going to have to wait this one out.

I was useless for the rest of the day. I couldn't stay in my office. My room was right across the hall from where the snake was housed. Consequently, I roamed the school all day with my eyes glued to the floors, ceilings and walls. I felt sorry for the teachers that had to stay in their rooms, especially on the fourth floor. My hope was that the snake went to another floor to live. Any floor would be my choice as long as it left the fourth floor. That day I left the school still unsure of what my options would be if they could not find that snake.

That evening after dinner I received a call from Action Jackson. He seemed to still have the giggles, but thank goodness, it was nothing like what he had in school. After a few more chuckles he said,

"I thought you would be happy to know that the snake has been found. It seems he found a hiding place right there in the lab and never even left the room. Observing your reaction to the news when it was first announced, I figured you would prefer to hear the good news tonight and not have to wait until the morning."

Subsequent to giving him the biggest "thank you," I hung up the phone. I was ecstatic. I felt like the weight of the world was lifted from my shoulders. That night I slept like a baby.

CHAPTER 45

One morning as I approached my school, I could see trouble looming in the distance. Pulling into a parking spot a block away, I strained my eyes to see if I could get an idea of what was happening. Emergency vehicles were everywhere. Police cars were blocking the intersections at the beginning and end of the block. Only ambulances were allowed to enter the immediate vicinity. My imagination ran wild wondering what could have occurred on such a gorgeous morning. Our vacation would begin in nine days. Everyone, and I do mean everyone, was looking forward to that glorious day when we could kiss Bradley Middle School farewell for a few months. I was hoping that nothing dreadful was happening with our students that could put a stressful ending to our school year.

"What happened?" asked a familiar voice from behind. Looking over my shoulder I recognized Joe, one of the security guards that patrolled the school. Shrugging, I gave him the benefit of my limited knowledge.

"Don't know, but it looks like something big. I count twelve police cars, three ambulances and two fire trucks. It seems like they called out the cavalry for this one."

"Tell me about it," as he spoke a frown appeared on his face. "Not even the President of the United States gets this much attention. From the looks I would say that somebody died. In fact, maybe more than one person might have "bit the dust."

I had to agree with him. Whatever happened was obviously catastrophic. Together we walked down the block and as we crossed the street, we were stopped by a policeman before reaching the opposite side.

"Sorry, street's closed," he remarked as he stretched out his arm to block our path.

"Officer," I began speaking in a low voice, "What in the world happened here? I'm one of the deans in the school."

I was hoping that this volume of speaking would generate an atmosphere of confidentiality. People tend to open up and be more candid if they feel you can be discreet. It worked! Following my lead, the officer lowered his voice to a whisper.

"There are two dead bodies in that house with the yellow tape. This tragedy appears to be a lovers' triangle. They say the female was entertaining her boyfriend when her husband came home early from work. He caught them in bed and flipped out. Neighbors said they could hear his wife and her boyfriend pleading for their lives. Our department received a 911 call. Unfortunately, the neighbors waited until they heard gun shots before calling us. By then it was too late to help anyone."

"What a tragedy," I said remembering my experience with the Jamez family. "It's a shame that people don't want to get more involved in trying to help their fellow man. Neighbors don't get involved when there is domestic violence and physical assaults taking place." As I spoke, he was shaking his head in agreement. I continued, "They bury their heads and don't come up for air until it's too late. It appears that most people feel that other folks' problems are not their business."

The cop interrupted, "You're right about that! I overheard one neighbor say to another some mess like . . . every man should handle his own home. I'm sure he never considered that a call ten minutes earlier might have saved two lives. Two people dead and one going to prison; probably for the rest of his life if he isn't put on death row. I just don't understand it."

He was shaking his head in disbelief as his voice trailed away. Officer West (that's what his badge read) was really muttering to himself when he made that last statement. I could barely hear what he said. He was right, though. Residents of most neighborhoods did not get involved.

Silently we watched the EMS workers take two bodies out of the building. Shortly afterward, they brought a man out in handcuffs. His head was hanging down as if he didn't want anyone to see his face. I can't blame him. I wouldn't want anyone to see my face either. But it was too late to hide. By tomorrow morning his picture would be plastered all over the news. As they put the man into the police car, photographers from the media were busily positioning their bodies in order to achieve the perfect shot. I saw many of our students in the crowd and I wondered how this would impact their existence. Hopefully, those observers who might be headed down the wrong path would think about today's tragic events and make a U turn in their lives before reaching the point of no return.

One hour after we came to school we were allowed on the block and into the building. The atmosphere was solemn for the staff as well as the students. Everywhere you went conversations of this morning's disaster could be heard. I listened to accounts that some of our students knew the people involved in the incident.

Three o'clock finally arrived. Everyone was happy to see the day end. I don't believe this has ever happened before, but Bradley Middle School was completely empty within ten minutes.

CHAPTER 46

"Oh what a beautiful morning, oh what a beautiful day, la la la la la la laaa laaa, everything's going my way." As I drove to work, I found myself singing that song. Too bad I couldn't recall most of the words. But the ones I remembered took me back many years to my childhood. Once again pleasant memories of my mother popped up. Mom could always find a happy song to sing even when depressing situations were staring her in the face. She would say, *"Singing will make the hurt go away."* Usually, she was right. Today was the last day of school and that made me want to sing and shout. Two months off for an educator was nothing to sneeze at and it definitely required a musical celebration. Like mom envisioned, my spirits were beginning to soar already.

Since January, both students and teachers relentlessly counted the days to their liberation. Even though most teachers loved their jobs, by now the constant stress that accompanied many of our positions had taken its toll. That meant, like the students, we were very anxious for the month of June to arrive. Today, happy sounds were heard throughout the building.

Students laughing with teachers and teachers joking with students were apparent on every floor. This was one of the few days in each year that the student body and the faculty were on the same page. Students who disliked their teachers all year would suddenly refer to the same teachers as "cool." Contrary to their prior letters of complaints, teachers who had students that were considered "royal pains in the asses" were unexpectedly now labeled as being just a little rambunctious, active, or spirited. As you can see, everything and anything is relative. One thing I'm sure about was that both groups were glad to be away from the other, even if was only for a short while.

I stood in my office and looked around, not sure of what my next course of action should be. Still debating on whether to accept the dean's position next year, I decided to wait until I resolved my personal conflict before emptying my desk. My immediate future was bright with time off to relax and lower my stress level. There was plenty of time to make a decision. After all, the dean's job might not seem as difficult to me after my extended rest. So, I decided I would "let my decision ride" until September. Besides, I was looking forward to today's end of the term party that my colleagues had been planning for the past month. Earlier I peeked into the teachers' cafeteria where everything looked festive and a delicious aroma was emitted. I handed my home-made cake to Mrs. Woods, teacher in charge of setting up the goodies, and headed for the fourth floor. We planned to get an early start on our party since the students had a half day and were leaving at noon.

The ringing of my phone brought me back to my surroundings. Now, what do they want from me at this hour? As I answered the phone on the third ring, I looked at my watch. I noticed it was only nine minutes to ten in the morning.

"Mrs. Lawson," Mr. Ballentine's heavy voice boomed over the phone, "we have a problem!"

What does he mean by *we*, I wondered. However, keeping my thoughts to myself I answered instead, "What kind of problem do *we* have?" I emphasized the *we* when I responded.

"We have a fight developing. I should really refer to this fight as a massacre as it's six against one."

Now . . . I was fully attentive! He began to tell me a story that was simply outrageous.

"We have six eighth grade girls that graduated last week. They are back and are waiting outside to beat up a seventh grader at dismissal. I was informed by some students that the girls said there wasn't anything that we could do to them since they had already graduated. I could call the police, but I feel her enemies would still manage to get to her before she reaches her house. Anyway, all the police would probably do is force them to move from in front of the building. That wouldn't solve the problem. They would just find another location to ambush her. There are four blocks in-between her house and the school. They could easily trap her along that route."

Mr. Ballentine paused, which gave me the opportunity to ask him what he planned to do about the situation.

"I've got an idea. How about you drive her home now? They won't expect her to leave this early and I don't think they know the staff is aware of their plans. You could drive your car to the back of the school. That way we could sneak her out the back door directly into your car without being noticed. In a few minutes I'll have her teacher secretly give her the report card and send her down to my office with a phony folder. What are your thoughts on this plan?"

"I think that it will work! I'll meet you at the back door in twenty minutes."

After hanging up the phone, I swiveled my chair around and looked out the window. Like he said, six girls were across the street just hanging out, obviously waiting for someone. Wasting no time, I got my pocketbook and headed for the stairs. My car was parked at the side of the building. Luckily it could not be seen by the group out front. I drove it around to the back of the school without being noticed and waited. Shortly afterward, Mr. Ballentine came out holding Kimberly by her arm. She got into the back seat where we had her lie down so that she would not be seen. Then, for additional security, I covered her with a blanket that I always carried in the trunk of my car.

CHAPTER 47

On the drive to her house, Kimberly told me the rest of the story that Mr. Ballentine didn't know.

"It's all about this boy I'm seeing, Ms. Lawson. He happens to be the boyfriend of Jackie, one of the girls waiting out front. I didn't know this when he asked me to go to the movies. But if I did know it, it wouldn't have made a difference to me. I still would have gone out with him. Anyway, last night Jackie called me and told me to stay away from her man. I told Jackie that she could go to hell 'cause he's my man now. Before she hung up the phone, she told me that she would settle up with me today. Ms. Lawson, you and Mr. Ballentine didn't have to worry. She doesn't scare me. I could handle all of those bitches by myself. I'm waiting for them to mess with me. I've something for all of them."

Looking at her in my rear-view mirror, I believed her. I knew she would probably try to take them on. However, I don't know how far she would get with six girls. But no doubt about it, she would definitely make an impression on the pack. And what did she mean by saying, "she had something for all of them." I didn't dare ask even though I felt I knew. It was most likely a weapon of some kind. Kimberly stayed under my radar and never had to come to my office, but I heard quite a lot about her from Janell St. Patrick. I knew she had a reputation of being tough and was known to have whipped a few butts. I had also heard gossip that she would pull a knife if she felt threatened. Most likely those six girls knew that she could be dangerous. That's why Jackie brought so many friends with her. And I would bet that they were carrying weapons too. It looks like we dodged another bullet today. I'm glad we got her away from the school. If we didn't, we could have been facing another incident on the last day of school, and this one would have been a whopper.

By now we had reached her house. Her mom came out to meet us and thanked me for helping her daughter. She said that Mr. Ballentine had called informing her of the dilemma Kimberly was facing. To avoid any more problems, she was sending her daughter out of state to her grandmother for a while until everything calmed down. As I drove back to school I wondered if those young ladies would ever leave Kimberly alone. If they were like most girls, they would carry this grudge for eternity.

When I arrived back at the school, I was fortunate to have my same parking space waiting for me. That was good because I didn't want to pass those girls while looking for another spot. It wouldn't help anyone, above all me, if they knew I took Kimberly out of the building, especially since I had a new car parked outside for them to ruin. I entered the school by the same door that I left from. Mr. Ballentine was waiting for me in his office. I told him what had transpired with her mother. At the same moment we both remembered our unwelcomed visitors and simultaneously turned to look out the office window at the girls still waiting across the street. Their presence told us that they were not aware our young lady was gone.

I went back to my office and finished locking up before going down early to the teacher's cafeteria. I must confess that all the good food was calling my name. I could hear their chatter all the way to the fourth floor. As you would expect I didn't want to disappoint those delicious dishes. So, without any more delay, I immediately succumbed to their alluring chant.

School for the students ended at twelve o'clock. By twelve fifteen all students had left the building eager to start their vacations. Staff members began to join me in the teachers' cafeteria. Of course, I had a thirty-minute head start. It was a very tasty and enjoyable party.

I left the school at two o'clock. The six girls were still waiting across the street. They had called for reinforcements in the form of three additional girls who were waiting at the back of the school just in case Kimberly tried to escape. I guess they figured she was still hiding out somewhere in the building. They were too late. She was home packing and would be leaving town the next morning. My sympathy went out to Kimberly, but my main concern was whether she would ever be able to come back and live in peace with those girls in her neighborhood. It would help if her family moved away from the area. But I doubt that would happen. I was told that Kimberly's parents owned their home for over ten years and were not presently in a position to make any financial changes in their lives. As I drove home still troubled about the events of the day, it was gratifying to observe the children happily playing with their friends along the way.

Vacation began today and throughout the city children of all ages were celebrating their freedom. All were engaged in fun except those angry girls stationed in front of the school. They didn't seem to notice or even care about the fun their peers were having. All they wanted was revenge. They wasted their entire day just watching and waiting. As I entered my block eagerly looking forward to beginning my own vacation, I couldn't help but wonder how long Jackie and her friends were going to squander precious time hanging around waiting for their rival. Kimberly was safe for now; however, in the months to come she might be facing the wrath of those same girls upon returning to her neighborhood. If today's circumstances were any indication of future events, then I can't help but wonder about the coming year and what problems would be in store for Bradley Middle School.

www.ingramcontent.com/pod-product-compliance
Lightning Source LLC
LaVergne TN
LVHW040150080526
838202LV00042B/3098